Demitrius

ERIKSON BROTHERS BOOK 4

KATHI S. BARTON

This is a work of fiction. Names, characters, places, and incidents are products of the author's imagination or are used fictitiously and are not to be construed as real. Any resemblance to actual events, locations, organizations, or persons, living or dead, is entirely coincidental.

World Castle Publishing, LLC
Pensacola, Florida
Copyright © 2025 Kathi S. Barton
Hardback ISBN: 9798283913964
Paperback ISBN: 9798891264083
eBook ISBN: 9798891264090
First Edition World Castle Publishing, LLC, May 19, 2025
http://www.worldcastlepublishing.com

Cover: Cover Designs by Karen
Editor: Karen Fuller

Chapter 1

Mandy was waiting to have her stitches taken out when a young woman came into the room looking like she was going to pop her kid at any moment. It took her a few seconds only, though, to not care for the woman. She was demanding and privileged acting.

"You need to get up out of that chair, young man. I've always sat there, and it's the most comfortable one in the room." Then she snapped her fingers at him. "Hello, pregnant woman here. Don't make me get pissy with you about a stupid chair."

"Then sit someplace else. I was here first." She huffed at the man, then tried to sit in the chair anyway, shoving the man to the side until he got up or she sat directly on him. What Ms. Privileged didn't count on was his being bigger than her. "What the hell are you doing? Are you insane? I'm sitting here."

"I'm pregnant. Or are you too stupid to know that?" The man looked her up and down and said that she was stupid as well. "Do you have any idea who I am? I'm going to have my husband arrest you when you're out on the streets. You'll have so many fines that you'll never see your paycheck. Is that what you want?"

"I'm a cop too. And I do know who you're married to. Donny isn't even the father of this kid, and you both know it. Now be a good little girl and find yourself another seat, and leave me to my own."

Ms. Privileged huffed again. But instead of moving to another seat, she simply stood in front of the man while he seemed to be ignoring her. It was funny how stubborn she was. He was as well, but at least he was justified in his stubbornness.

When her name was called, she was slightly disappointed that she'd not get to see what happened when one of their names was called back. Would she feel triumphant and sit in the chair, or would she be called back first, and it was all for nothing on her part? Oh well, she'd take entertainment when she could get it.

"These look really good, but I'm going to take my time pulling them out. It's a large cut, and I don't want you to have it leave a big scar for you." She thanked Misty, Doctor Keller's nurse. "The doc is going to want to see you in a couple of weeks just to make sure that you're healing all right."

She wished that Locke could have taken them out since he'd been the one who had put them in. But he'd been working in the emergency department for the last month since he'd become a doctor and hadn't had time to work her in. Nor did he have the sort of equipment at home to work on her. He told her that he'd be more prepared next time. She hoped there wouldn't be a next time.

Trying to ignore her skin being pulled while the stitches were being pulled out, she thought of the list that Zander, Locke's brother, had given her if she wanted to try and adopt her nephews. They'd found another relative to take them in, but she couldn't get past the background check that the county had done on her.

Her name was Georgie Jameson, the same as the boys, but she had an arrest record that was about a mile long. After Georgie's brother, Samuel, had killed their mother in a drunken rage, they didn't want the same thing to happen to the boys. It was bad enough that they'd seen her killed by him; making them go to the same sort of person wouldn't be right on any level.

"Mandy? Are you all right?" She said she was just thinking. "You really zoned out there on me. I was worried that you were really hurting."

"No, not at all. You did a good job." At least she hoped so. While the scar was ugly and still very pink looking, it was better than the open, gaping wound that she'd had there a month ago. Samuel had cut her with a knife while she was trying her best to keep the two little boys safe. They'd come to mean the world to her. "What do I have to do to take care of it? I know that someone mentioned that I'm to keep it out of the sun."

"Yes, I'll give you some instructions for wound care before you leave. Now all you have to do is see the Doc and you'll be free to go." Sounded good to her. Maybe she'd get to see the end of the fight in the lobby. "You have a good day, Mandy, and be careful."

She and the boys had been living with August and his wife, Jack, since the night that their mother had been killed. Her sister had married Samuel about ten years ago and had had Teddy first. Then, a couple of years later, Martin had come along. Besty had been a good mom, but she always thought that she should have left Samuel after the first time she'd been beaten bad enough to end up in the hospital, about a week after they were married. But then she'd not have Teddy and Martin, and Besty always told her that was worth it all.

Walking back to the house she was staying at, she decided to find out if there were any places to rent yet. She'd been going by the real estate office daily for the past three weeks, and they'd had nothing. Nothing that she could afford anyway.

Now, with her first check coming in, surprised

at how much it was, she thought that finding a place for the three of them was going to be much easier. Plus, it was on the list of things that she had to do that Zander had given her to make it so she could adopt the boys when it went to court. She needed to establish someplace where they could live on their own.

The list wasn't all that long, but it was things that she was having trouble thinking anyone would care about. What did it matter if she ate out often without the boys? Or that she didn't have reliable daycare for them when she went to work. Mostly she took them with her, and it hadn't been an issue. But she'd do each and every thing on the list just to be able to take care of the three of them in one place.

"I do have a place. I was hoping you'd come by today." The woman, Izzy was her name, grabbed her coat and keys, and said that she'd take her by there now. "He's a good person to rent from. I think you know him, Demitruis Erikson. He's one of the Erikson men who live around here. It's a three-bedroom and has two baths. You'll love it."

As they drove to the place, she tried her best not to get her hopes too high for it. While it sounded perfect, there could be a plethora of things wrong with it that would get her into trouble with the county. They'd have to inspect it as well, she thought she'd read.

"It's in a good neighborhood, too. Not far from his restaurant either." Mandy told Izzy that she'd not met this brother as he'd been working on getting his place opened. "He does work hard. They all do, for that matter. And they all take care of each other, too."

Mandy knew that as well. They took care of strangers who showed up on their doorsteps like they were family as well. She knew that to be true firsthand. As they were pulling into the drive of the house, all she could think about was how beautiful it looked with all the trees. She could almost see her raking up leaves and the boys jumping in them. The fenced-in back yard was an added bonus, too.

Mandy toured the house three times before she got around to asking what the rent was. She had to have her tell her four times the amount, as it just seemed too low for her to be right. Then she mentioned that the other services for the house, such as water, sewage, and cable, were included. The man must be certifiable if he was letting it go for this low.

"I'll take it."

After handing her the visa that she'd just gotten the other day, Izzy said she'd call it in. Then she remembered the county, and it was then that Izzy told her that the house had only been just inspected for her, and she was all right. It occurred to her that someone was setting this up for her, but she didn't voice that.

If the Eriksons were helping her, she wasn't going to look a gift horse in the mouth. They were more than likely tired of her hanging around their homes while not being related to them in any way.

Signing the paperwork once they were in the office again, she was almost too excited to tell the boys what she'd done. Then something else occurred to her. She had not one stick of furniture nor anything personal to put in the place. She almost wanted to sob right then. What a fool she'd been.

Walking home, trying not to be too upset about the blunder that she'd made. She decided that she was going to ask for the help that had been given to her by each of the family members that she'd met. They all told her to come to them when she needed something, and she was going to do it. All she needed was enough money to get herself some kitchen supplies and two beds for the boys. She could sleep on the floor until she got herself something else, she decided.

Then her list of things that she needed got longer with each step that she took. Towels. Food. They'd need to have a shower curtain as well as bathing supplies. Once she was in the house again, she burst into tears when Jack had asked her what was wrong.

It all came tumbling out. "I don't know what I was thinking. I know what I was thinking about that Demitrius was helping me fund the place, and I'd not even met him. Now I've signed the lease agreement, and I don't have anything to make it work." She listed only a few things that she'd thought of on her way home. "Not to mention, how the heck am I supposed to be able to care for the boys when I can't even care for myself?"

"Are you finished whining?" She told Jack that she'd not been whining by stating facts. "Whining. We'll help you. We're all rooting for you to—why are you shaking your head? I said we'd help you. I didn't ask you if you wanted us to help you. Now, here's what we're going to do. We're going to go and measure rooms, you and I, and then the others will meet. Stop shaking your head, no. You'll get a headache, and that won't bode well when you tell Teddy and Martin you have a place for them."

"It's going to be a lot of money. And even making the kind of money that I am now, it'll be forever before I can pay you back." Jack put her hands on her hips and tapped her toe. "You might scare the rest of them with that look, but I've stared down a man holding a gun to my forehead. You don't come back from that quickly."

"He really did that?" She nodded. "I'm sorry. I didn't know, but that doesn't change the fact that we're going to help you out. Really, it's what we do. And someday you can do the same thing when someone comes to you needing help."

"If someone comes to me for help, I'm going to have to refer them to you guys, I don't have a pot to piss in right now." She waved her off, pulling out her cell phone. Before she could object, even if she thought that she could have, they were on their way to the house with the boys and armed with tape measures and notepads. These people were beyond pushy, she realized.

The house seemed warmer now that she was going to be living in it. The boys, especially Martin, were excited that he'd still have his own room. He loved his brother, but he snored, he told them. Teddy was excited to have his own back yard, something that he'd asked for when she'd told them they were going to be all living together. The other two women showed up about the time they had finished measuring each room and writing down the colors of the walls, most of them creamy white, so that they knew what to work with. She didn't know what that meant; she only needed supplies and a couple of beds for the kids.

"I don't need that right now." It had become her litany for things put in her cart while they were out. It didn't matter if she didn't need it right away; she would eventually, and they were going to buy it. She was also making sure that she thanked them for all the stuff in the carts, not one or two carts so far, but three.

"I can get that with my next paycheck" was something else that went unheard…or ignored, she didn't know which. But they did a good job of finding her the best deals. A mental running total was making her sick with anxiety.

"You look pinched." Thanking Martin for pointing that out, he cocked his little head at her and she waited for what he'd say next. "You need something to eat, I bet. I'm starving and I already ate my stash."

She'd noticed that the whole family did that. Even the little ones had something to munch on when they went out. Locke usually had two or three granola bars or a couple of apples. He forever had a bottle of water on him, the same as his brothers. She did wonder what sort of childhood they'd had that would make them so afraid of being hungry.

"You know that's a wonderful idea." Shipley— her last name, she assumed that everyone called her by winked at her. "I'm hungry too, and I handed over my last cookie to Alex. All right, we'll pay for this and go get some lunch. I didn't realize how late it was."

"It's only two in the afternoon. How about we get something and take it to my place now, and I can get this stuff put away while the boys eat something." She told her that they'd not filled her pantry yet. "I didn't know that I had a pantry. And I'm sure you know it."

"You're very stubborn, aren't you?" She just

stared at her open mouthed. "Close your mouth, deary, the men are coming. They'll get this sorted out, and we can all dine together."

After getting kisses from their spouses, she stood there thinking that she was going to put up a fuss about them buying groceries too. But when Teddy took her hand, telling her in a very loud whisper that he wanted to eat breakfast in his own house tomorrow, she couldn't turn him down. As it was right now, she was in debt to the family for thousands of dollars, and she really didn't have anything in the cupboards.

Lunch was fun. She finally got to meet Demitrius, Demi, as everyone called him, and the boys were having a good time with the other children at the table. August had five kids, and he and Jack seemed to be pros at keeping them entertained and happy. The others pitched in when they were needed, and she loved it all.

"I'm glad you like the house." She told Demi that she was looking forward to living there with the boys. "They'll have fun too. There are a lot of kids on that street who are about the same age as them. I think there are a lot of people your age there as well."

"You make it sound like I'm old. I'm only twenty-five." He turned pink, and she felt stupid for embarrassing him. "I'm sorry. I didn't mean to embarrass you. My mouth gets ahead of my mind at times. Forgive me."

"Nothing to forgive you for. I thought it was funny, too. And I'm only twenty-seven. So not too far off. You should come to the restaurant when you have time. Dinner will be on me."

Her mind, never in a good place, imagined Demi spread out on a table with food all over him for her to eat. Now she was the one embarrassed and told him that she'd love that. Thankfully, Martin drew his attention away from her, and she had a moment to rethink where her mind had gone.

~*~

Demi enjoyed the time with his family. Had he been open today, he would have entertained them in his place. *The Crockery Pot* wasn't open on Mondays or on Tuesday afternoon. It gave the people who worked for him time to do their own personal things without having to miss work. Besides, as busy as he'd been since opening, he didn't think that having a couple of days closed was going to break him.

The woman, Mandy, was nice. She embarrassed easily, and he thought that was adorable. He had no desire to leap into a relationship like his brothers had. He might take her out or something, get to know her, and decide that she wasn't for him. Or if she was for him, he'd take his time and get to know not just her but the boys she was trying to adopt as well. He didn't know anything about their circumstances and was happy to keep it that way for the time being.

"I didn't say I wanted to date you." He looked at Mandy, wondering if she read minds or something. "You mumble when you're thinking. I have my life just the way I want it too, so back off and we'll both be great."

"I'm sorry." She turned away from him and while it pissed him off a little he knew that it was no less than he deserved. "I'm truly sorry that I thought those things. If you knew how my brothers seemed to just fall in love with their wives, you'd understand where I'm coming from."

"I don't, nor do I care. It's none of my business." She looked at him again. "Look. You just keep to your side of the street, and I'll do the same for mine. And if you think to make me leave the house now that I've said I have no desire to date you, then you'll be in for a rude awakening. I'll sue you for breach of contract. I've signed the lease and have paid my deposit. There'll be no raising my rent either. It's in the contract for one year."

"I never said that I'd do that." He was getting angrier by the moment and had to try to reign in his temper or make a scene. "Look, I was thinking things to myself. It's not my fault that you listened in when it was none of your business. I don't want to have anything to do with you either. You're not nice."

She turned fully away from him, showing him her back. Before he could reach up and pull her around, he looked at his family. Jack was staring at him like she dared him to do it. What? Well, he wasn't sure, but he wasn't to touch Mandy.

Demi finished his meal in silence. He'd speak when asked something, but nothing more than that. His anger and temper, never right on the edge like they were right now, were making him ill with it. As soon as the check came, he grabbed it from the waitress and said he was leaving.

No one said anything to him. There were no begging him to stay. He felt his anger grow more when he was able to walk away without a word from anyone, especially Mandy. He did feel bad as he was paying, realizing that he'd been rude to the staff, but he'd make it up in the tip. He didn't know what was bothering him so much about her hearing what he'd been mumbling about, but he wanted to go home and beat on his heavy bag for a few hours. Or days. He was just in the kind of mood that would have gotten him in trouble when he'd been younger, much like his father's temper.

That cooled him off right away. He never wanted to be compared to that bastard. Not even by himself. Stretching his neck several times so that when someone slapped him on the back, he nearly snarled at them to leave him alone. He was glad that he'd not when he noticed that it was his brother Knox.

"What's up?" He asked him what he was talking about. "You nearly bit that woman's head off earlier than the two of you were like strangers all of the sudden. So again, what's up?"

"It's my fault." He realized that it was too. All his fault. "I said some things under my breath and she heard me."

"You were mumbling." He asked him how he knew that. "You talk out loud when you're stressed out. It comes out like you're mumbling, but it's really you just talking low. I think that Zander does it too. So how bad was it? She's mad at you, and I'm assuming you said something not so nice about her."

"I don't want to fall in love with her right away." Knox just eyed him. "Well, everyone else has, and I don't want to even date her for fear that we'll be something to each other. I have enough going on in my life that I don't need another complication like a woman with two kids to mess with."

"Wow, you really did a number on her then." He laughed, but it sounded like he was angry too. "I don't blame her for being pissed off. You? You said some pretty harsh things, even under your breath, about a near stranger, if you said all that. Christ, man. What's wrong with you having some fun by going out? And it's doubtful to me that you're going to find yourself anyone if you have an attitude like that."

When his brother left him standing there, he could see him sitting by Mandy. She didn't warm up to him right away, but she was speaking to him. Going out the door, feeling the need to break something, he got into his car and had to take in several deep breaths and let them out slowly before he thought he could take a chance and drive. Christ, he thought, this was a royal fuck up and he didn't have anyone to blame but himself.

By the time he was home, he had four messages and two missed calls. All from his family. He'd gone there to help with packing things in trucks, then taking them to Mandy's home, but he thought for sure that it would go better if he wasn't there at all. He knew that being around Mandy right now would cause a lot of trouble. None that he was looking for, that's for sure.

He ended up in his basement with his exercise equipment, pounding on the bag for about ten minutes, when his phone rang again. He'd told them all that he'd been feeling off and didn't want to help out, but apparently that wasn't an excuse enough to keep them from calling him. He answered the phone on about the fifth ring and barked his name into the phone.

"What did you do?" He asked Shipley what

she meant. "You've hurt Mandy. She's not saying anything, but in the words of Teddy, you looked about as pinched as Mandy did when we got back to her place to put things away. So again, what did you do to her?"

"Nothing. What did she say I did?" She told him that she wasn't saying anything either. "Good. At least she knows when to shut up."

As soon as the words left his mouth, he knew his mistake. But there was no taking it back now, and he listened to Shipley beat him up with words while he took it. When she seemed to be winding down, he asked her if she was about finished, he had shit to do.

"You bastard." He hurt knowing that he'd hurt her too. "So, are you going to start drinking soon? I'm told that all the fucking bastards—your father included, do that." When she hung up the phone on him, he did the only thing that he could think of, which was to throw his phone across the room and hit the wall. It was shattered even as it dropped to pieces onto the floor.

"Now I need a phone." Getting on the treadmill, he was going about as fast as he could make it without killing himself when someone knocked on his door. Not answering it made him feel like he'd live a bit longer, especially if it was August, Jack's husband and his brother. Zoning out on the treadmill, he was nearly startled off it when his brother knocked hard on the glass door that led out into the back yard from the basement doors. Christ, would no one leave him in peace?

"I'm not in the mood." He tried blocking the door so that his brother would get the hint and leave him alone. Fat lot of good it did him as he just shoved him out of the way and came in anyway. "I didn't hang up on your wife; she did me."

"I know that, dumbass. She sent me over here to see if you were all right. I didn't know what was going on any more than she did until I talked to Knox. He's worried about you, too. Said you were flying off the handle for no reason. Just because you don't want to date Mandy or something like that."

"I don't, not that it's any of your business." He said it wasn't but that he'd hurt Mandy. "Then she should have been minding her own business and not listening to me. I apparently mumble when I'm thinking, and she heard things that were private."

Even to his own ears, that sounded lame. Grabbing a towel, suddenly realizing how sweaty he was, he asked his brother if he was going to leave soon. All he did was sit down on one of the many chairs that he'd gotten at garage sales for cheap.

"You want to talk about it?" He told him no, not at all. "I think you do. Before you break something else down here."

"What are you talking about?" he nodded toward the heavy bag that was spilling sand onto the floor even as he stood there. "I did that a week ago."

"Sure you did. And it's just now leaking out. Anything else you broke a week ago that you want to talk about?" Demi sat down in the other chair that matched the ugly one that his brother was sitting in. "I've never seen you this pissed off before. Knox mentioned that you had a bit of beer on your breath. Are you drinking too?"

"I had half a can of beer left over from cooking hot dogs for the restaurant, and I spit it out when I tasted it. I won't drink any more than any of the rest of us will. And Jack said I was acting like our father. I'm not that mean."

August didn't say anything, but he did stare at him. Leaning back in his own seat, he wondered where all this anger was coming from. He wasn't really stressed out, not as much as he could have been. Looking at his brother, he was surprised when he snored. Christ, he'd fallen asleep in seconds. He felt his temper flare about that, too.

But instead of acting on it, like smacking his brother around until he woke up, Demi decided to take a shower. As he was getting under the hot spray, he realized how much he was telling his crew how sorry he was too. And just last week he'd made one of them cry. Something was wrong with him, and he didn't know what to do about it.

Getting out, he was marginally better but not perfectly calm. Going into the outer area where August was, he found him on his cell phone. Getting dressed in something comfy, he opted for a pair of shorts that had seen better days as well as some socks that he thought were clean. August was getting off his cell when he was pulling on his shirt over his head.

"That was Locke. He said to tell you to behave yourself. I told him that I think you were from now on." He pointed out that he wasn't five. "Then don't act like it. If you don't want to be treated as a child, then act like you're an adult."

"I'm trying. I don't know what's wrong with me." He looked at his brother when he stood up. "I've been snapping at people for two weeks now. I think that if I make one more person cry, then I'm going to be out of staff. I just can't seem to get my shit together enough to keep out of the doghouse. I feel like shit all the time nowadays."

"Have you been to the doctor? I mean, you must know that this isn't you?" He said that he'd not been, but he didn't think he was ill. "Well, something is wrong. You're going to have to apologize to Mandy and the rest of the family for the stunts you pulled today. It would be better all the way around if you were to tell them that you're working on what's wrong. I, myself, think that you're working too hard. How many hours a week are you spending at the restaurant?"

"Sometimes as much as twenty hours a day." August asked him if he was serious. "Yeah, I just realized that when I was in the shower. I'm there nearly all the time. I even have a cot there."

"You're going to go there with me now. Call your employees and tell them that you're giving them a week off with pay. Then you're going to come home with me and cuddle the kids. They'll do wonders for your anger. Then, after a week if you're better, I'll think about allowing you — don't you dare tell me no, Demitrius Alan Erickson. This is some serious business you're messing with. Either do it or I will. I don't want to lose you to some kind of heart issues." He knew his brother was right, but it didn't make him feel any better. He agreed to follow his brother into the place and close it down. It was only for a week. He'd be able to do that, Demi was sure.

However, the closer he got to the restaurant, the more he was regretting taking his brother up on his offer. There was just too much riding on him making a good showing of his first place.

Chapter 2

Mandy wasn't sure she was ever going to get everything put away. While the kitchen looked big when it was empty. With a table and four chairs, the trash can and the cupboards full, it seemed as tiny as the bathroom was. Even that took on a smaller appearance when she had the linens filled out in there as well.

"Can I have some carrots?" Mandy told Martin she thought there was a bag full of them on the counter. "Thanks. I'm going to eat them real careful at the table. I don't want to mess things up, in case they come back and get the stuff they gave us."

"Oh, honey, they won't do that. You can be as messy as you want. Though I'm going to make you clean it up when you're done." She tousled his hair and told him that she loved him. "See if your brother wants anything. I thought for our first night here we'd order pizza and see how long it takes for us to get it. Deal?"

The house looked like they'd lived there for decades instead of about five hours. After the family left, having set up the furniture as well as the beds, including one for herself, she was ready to call it a day. But there were groceries still on the counter that had been left, as well as a few things that she said she'd get put together, like the vacuum cleaner and the coffee table. It was all lovely furniture, but she was still wondering how she was going to be paying them all back. They spent several thousand dollars on her home, and she wasn't even related to them. And there were things that she still needed to get, like a coffee maker.

None of them drank coffee, so they'd not thought of getting her one. She had told them that she only had a cup a couple of times a week, so she thought it was a waste of money. But right now, she'd give anything for a nice hot cup of the stuff just to calm her down. She felt as if she'd been running all day long. And she had.

At a quarter to seven, they were having pizza when the doorbell rang. Mandy was ready to tell anyone at the door they were all right, the neighbors had been coming over to meet them, but when she looked into the peephole, she couldn't believe it was Demi. She spoke to him without opening the door.

"What do you want?" He laughed and told her that he wanted to apologize to her. "I accept and now go away. I'm having a meal with the boys."

"Please let me in. My family is going to be checking in with me to see how it went over, and I don't want to have any more trouble with them." She opened the door quickly, hoping to knock his head around when she did. Instead, he smiled at her. "Is that a Creno's pizza? Christ, I've not had one of them in years."

As he went by her, she was handed another pizza box, this one from Adornetto's Pizza. She'd heard of them, of course, but hadn't been to the larger town to get one. There was a bag sitting atop the box, and she took it to the table with the other pizza to ask him what he was doing.

"He's gonna eat with us. I invited him." She wanted to ask when that happened, but she only sat down to have her own slice eaten. "He's my friend."

"All right, but next time, ask first. In the event there isn't enough for all of us." Glaring at Demi when he scarfed down two slices of pizza, she wondered if there was going to be enough now. "Are you taking the other box home?"

"No, it was my peace offering. Go ahead, have some of it." He chewed the hot slice up and smiled again. "There are salads, too. They make the best salads if you ask me. There are four of them in the bag. The dressing is on the side."

Her mouth watered for one of the salads as soon as she saw it. Lettuce, cheese, and tomatoes were on it, and she opened one up for the boys when they said they wanted to share. Demi had told her the dressing was homemade. It was the best she'd ever eaten, too. After eating hers, she noticed that the boys had as well, and Demi was putting his pizza on the table when she realized that the one that they'd gotten was gone. Christ, it had been nearly a whole pizza when she'd gone to the door. She was glad that she'd been able to snag a couple of pieces of the hot one.

The four of them managed to eat nearly three-quarters of the second pizza. It was mainly Demi, he explained how he'd been working out today and had forgotten to eat, but there was one salad left that she was going to take to work tomorrow for lunch if Demi didn't take it with him. The boys went off to their rooms, they were moving things around the way they wanted them, and she got up to clean up the table.

"I'm so sorry for the way that I treated you today. It was uncalled for and rude." She turned to look at him, and he grinned. "You're not going to accept it, are you?"

"I told you that I would, but that doesn't mean that I like you any better than before. You were rude and hurtful when I didn't do anything wrong." He said that he knew that, too. "Good. Now you can go."

She was ready to toss him out of the house when Martin came into the room to ask for his help. His bed was in the wrong place, and since he was going to help, then they should be able to move it where he wanted. It just so happened that she'd tried moving the bed earlier when Teddy had wanted help, and it was just too heavy for her to do.

It took them nearly three hours to get the beds in the right place. Teddy had had an idea that he wanted his bed across the room from the two windows in his room, but it took up space in front of the closet. Demi never pointed out the mistakes that they were making, but moved them like they wanted. Even though she had her own room, her bed hadn't been put together, and he did that too. It was handy to have him around when he wasn't insulting her, she supposed.

At nearly three in the morning, she was ready to go to bed. She still had to work tomorrow, too. The boys were going to be staying with Locke's wife, Alex, as she had chores for them to do, and they were excited about that. Mandy was going to be dead on her feet tomorrow; she just knew it.

Demi left them after her bed was together and told the boys that he'd go by Alex's home to see them. Mandy didn't know who was more excited about the meet-up: the boys or Demi. As soon as she locked the doors and checked on the boys, she went to her own bedroom and plopped onto the bed. She was out before she realized, too late, that she'd forgotten to change her clothing.

She was up before her alarm went off. Having woken up in her shoes and clothing, she decided to get an early start on the day. Almost as soon as she found the box of Jiffy to make pancakes, someone was at her door. It was Demi again. And he looked fresh as a daisy and ready to work again.

"I'd not realized that you'd have to work today when I got home. So I picked up some coffee for you and some donuts for the kids. They're going to need the sugar when they get to Locke's home. Alex is going to be working in the yard blowing up things for the holidays. I think she has about a dozen of them just for Halloween."

The boys were up and dressed as she was finishing up her coffee. On the way home, she was going to pick up a coffee machine so she'd be able to indulge when she needed it. She wasn't a coffee expert, but she did enjoy a good cup of it when she was really stressed or tired. Like she was right now.

The donuts were a huge hit. She even had herself a muffin that was in the box to go with her brew. As the boys were telling Demi how they slept, she was about half-listening. Today was going to be a long one if she had to work without another cup of coffee. She looked at Demi when he said her name.

"Are you all right with me taking them to Alex's home? I promise you I'll drive carefully." She asked him what he was doing. That she'd forgiven him. "I like the kids. We don't have to like one another, but I do love the kids."

"All right, but I have no desire to date anyone, especially you. No offence but like you, I have enough going on right now that I don't have any time for myself, much less stroking an ego as large as yours seems to be." If she'd not been looking at him, she might have missed the flare of anger. It was there and gone quickly. "I don't want to fight with you here either. This is our home, even though you own it, and I want peace and quiet here, not just for me but for the boys, too. They've had enough stress in their lives without you being all pissed off all the time."

"It's no excuse, but I was working too hard. My brother made me close up my restaurant for a week so that I could get some rest. Last night, after leaving here, I slept better than I have in over a month, even though it was only for a few hours. I'm sorry, and I'll keep telling you that until you believe me. I never should have taken my temper out on you." She told him that no, he shouldn't have. His laughter made her own temper flare up. "I'm sorry, but I love the fact that you're not allowing me off the hook so quickly. Thank you for that."

After the boys were ready to go, Demi said he'd drop her off at the new offices too. She didn't want to be depending on someone, but she really was exhausted and needed something to perk her up. Getting to work on time was something that she strived for forever.

Getting the office open, she was surprised to see both Shipley and Jack come into the place. It was their offices and she only worked for them, but to see them in town at eight-thirty when they didn't need to be surprised her. She knew that they didn't laze around, even with all the money she'd heard they had, but it was nice to see them.

It took her nearly four hours to get the program running that they were going to use for the elderly when they opened up for classes. The ordering app for stores meant that anyone could order their groceries or other things in town and have them delivered directly to their home for a small fee. Or they could order and pick it up when it was ready. So far, she noticed that most of the users were using the pick-up part, and she thought that was wonderful.

The classes would be small. Only about four to the class. It would have been hard on her to have to teach more than that, as it was going to be hands-on for a while. The people who were coming in had to pay a small fee to the foundation for the classes, but it would also get them a discount on delivery from the stores. She loved that idea, too.

"I've got you something coming to your house

today. Since we didn't get you a coffee maker, I got one sent to you." She told Jack that she'd spent enough money; she could get herself a coffee machine. "I know that. But we all had so much fun helping you out yesterday that we've been looking around for other things like that we can do. You know, help people out."

"Well, I know that the washer and dryer are the handiest tools you could have gotten me. The boys have had to change into something cleaner at least twice a day; they get so muddy. I don't know what I'm going to do when they get bigger and their clothing doesn't fit in one load." They all laughed with her. "I do love being able to do laundry at home rather than lug it all over town to do it at a laundry mat. Are there any of those in town?"

"There used to be one called Browns, but it went out of business about ten years ago." Alex told her that the place just wasn't doing any business. "It was in the center where McDonalds is now. At the complete other end of the parking lot."

"If it was where you said it was, it's no wonder. That place is really off the beaten path, as the saying goes." She lived on the main street of town, about three doors down from the pizza place, as well as Demi's restaurant called the *Crockery Pot*. "Demi told me that he's closed up for a week to rest. I don't know how much rest he's going to be getting if he hangs out with my nephews too much. They had him lifting and toting things all night last night."

She expected them to say something about the argument that the two of them had gotten into, but they didn't. Nor did they ask her if she forgave Demi. She had, several times as a matter of fact, but they were talking about the programs that they wanted to teach, and she was glad for it. It was no one's business but hers and Demi's what went on between them.

As the day progressed, she didn't feel so tired. Mandy knew that by the time bedtime rolled around at their home, she was going to be hard-pressed into helping the boys with their own bedtime. School started back up in a few weeks, and both of them had been tested in the grades they were in, and she was proud of them. They were in second for Teddy and first for Martin. And since they lived right in town, she'd be able to walk them to school and then herself off to work. It was a good plan, she thought.

~*~

Samuel was sick of being told he was in jail for a long time. He wanted dates to go by, not something like weeks and days. Also, he had the boys to take care of, too. The little piss ants were going to pay for telling on him about beating their momma. She weren't worth spit if someone was to ask him about it, but he'd not meant to kill her.

His temper was usually at its worst when he was drinking. Not that he was sober all that much, but he was easy to rile up when he was into his fifth beer or so. She should have known better than to harp on him about a job when he was drinking. It just pissed him off that she had wanted him to get a job when she was getting all that welfare shit that she was getting. It was more than enough to get him some good beer and some money on the side, too.

After she'd go to the grocery store, he'd take the rest of the card money and turn it in for cash. There would be a lot of it, too. They were getting about nine hundred a month on the card, and that would mean that he'd be getting about half of it for himself. Christ, she'd pitch a bitch about not having any card left at the end of the month but he told her that she needed to spend it better. He'd asked her all the time, did he have to go with her to get things so she'd do it up right? Now she was gone.

With her being gone, he knew that he was going to have to figure out a few things from now on. One of them being the kids. He'd have to make sure that they got what they had coming, and that made him laugh. But he knew too that the house needed to stay in good condition or he'd lose out on that too. That was something that Besty told him all the time. The inspections could be at any time, with only a few hours to a couple of days' notice.

Not that he was supposed to be living in the house. He'd divorced Besty when she'd been big with the youngest. He didn't know if she knew it or not, he'd just tell her to sign off on the paperwork and then he'd go and file it for himself. It was why he wasn't supposed to be living in the house. She got a nicer one on account of him not being around all that much.

Because Besty was so good at the system stuff, he'd allowed her to get one of them cash cards too. It was to pay for babysitting and for transportation, since neither of them drove back and forth to the grocery or doctors' appointments. He took that from her, too.

Samuel would take the card with the promises of watching over the kids when she had something to do or had to go to her doctor's appointment. But he'd just send them in the yard and hope nobody stole them. Then again, he'd not lose all that much sleep over them being gone; they were a pest, always wanting something from him like food or water.

The one time that he'd put them in the back yard with a bowl of water and a package of crackers, she got powerful mad at him. She'd called the police on him for abusing his kids. She never did that again, and neither had he, but Samuel didn't understand why it was such a big deal. It got them fed and watered, didn't it?

"Your attorney is here. Do you want to speak to them here or in a room?" Samuel told him a room, anything to get out of the stuffy jail cell. He'd asked for a fan, but they didn't have any. He'd even offered to pay for one if they'd wait for the next check to come in from his wife. Even though she was dead, there were things that he needed, and he figured that since he was going to be responsible for his kids, then they'd just give him something. "Back against the wall, inmate, or you're not going anywhere."

"That's the stupidest rule ever, you know that, don't you? Why do I have to walk all the way back there only to walk all the way back to leave? What? You afraid of me or something?"

"You stink." Well, that was just rude, but he was out of his cell right now, so let it go. "Turn around with your hands out so that I can cuff you. Either that or you can go on sitting in here while there is nice air conditioning in one of the rooms."

Samuel kept his mouth shut with the officers. They're the ones that brought him his food, and he didn't want anyone spitting in it or, worse yet, not bringing him anything at all. He'd learned the hard way being in jail as much as he'd been that you don't fuck with the hands that feed you. They could be a mite on the stingy side, too, when it came to getting extras on your tray if you wanted them too.

The man sitting in the chair when he'd been brought looked like he'd just gotten out of grade school. Again, he didn't bring that up. He had learned that lesson, too. If they didn't like you for whatever reason, they'd not help you get out of jail sooner rather than letting you rot there. He sat back when he was chained to the table.

"My name is Richard McGee. No, I'm not going to be getting you a cell phone. I'm not going to be bringing you in dirty magazines or pictures for you to look at. I'm here to represent you, and that's all." He asked him about his food card money. "I'll check on that for you, but I wouldn't get my hopes up about getting one. You're in here because you murdered your ex-wife, and they tend not to give out food cards to convicted felons."

"I'm not convicted yet." He showed him his record, where he'd been caught stealing a car. "I thought that got wiped off your record when you did your jail time. Like a freebie or something."

"No, they don't do that. It's on your record for life. What do you have to tell me about Besty Jameson and the night that you killed her?" He said that he had allegedly killed her. "No, you confessed to the police when you were picked up. You even asked them if they'd turn their back so that you could finish the job and kill your sons, Theodore and Martin Jameson, minor children of yourself and your ex-wife."

"Oh yeah, I remember that now. No, I didn't mean that. You'll have to get them to not bring that up at the court thingy. I don't want to go back to prison. I have me two kids to watch over. That's why I'll be needing that stuff my wife got from the system. She was getting a right good amount too. About five grand a month when you count the house we was in." He made notes but didn't tell him he'd work on that. "What would it take for me to get myself a car to drive around? I have those two boys that I'm going to have to take to school."

"Get a job. When you get out of prison. I'm not saying that you'll get life, but I'd not count on you getting out anytime soon. You murdered someone, and that's not going to get you out of prison for a long time." He asked about his kids. "A Mandy Wilson is caring for them. She's been granted permission by the state so long as she has a job and a place for them to live."

"She ain't gonna take my kids no place. They're mine." He said that he'd murdered someone, and the courts more than likely wouldn't allow him near them, especially after saying that he wanted to kill them as well. "I was just joking around. You tell them that so that I don't have to spend extra time in here. You know as well as I do that they're better off with their parents than with some stranger. And she's not fit to have them around either."

"Do you know something about Ms. Wilson? From what I've been told, she's passed a background check and has had the Ericksons vouch for her. That's a good family. Also, she was your ex-wife's sister, wasn't she?" He said he didn't care about them. "Well then, tell me what you know about Ms. Wilson so that I can look into it. It can't be something that you make up, either. Whatever she's done, it has to be factual, not something that you've made up to get back at her."

"I'll think on that then." He hadn't even known that his wife had a sister until she showed up one day. And that was about the time that his wife had started getting uppity about things. Telling him that he needed to get a job so that she could get off of so much welfare. Didn't make any sense to him. Why wouldn't a person want to get all the freebie stuff she'd been getting? That was all on account of her sister putting her nose in where it didn't belong.

His attorney wasn't giving him the information that he wanted. According to him, he should plead guilty to get a lesser sentence than life without parole. He didn't want to be in jail at all, but he said that wasn't going to happen. Not with this. As it was now, if he would plead a deal, say he'd done it, then he'd get life and a parole hearing in about fifty years. Christ, he'd be too old to do anything if they did that to him.

"Look here. I want you to make it so I only have time served. I don't care how you do it, but you will or I'm going to do to you what I did to my wife. But I'll make you suffer more." He started gathering up his things and shoving them into his briefcase. "We ain't done here. You never did tell me what you were going to do to keep me from going to prison, and you will by god or I'm going to get out and take care of you."

"Goodbye, Mr. Jameson. I hope you have whatever life you deserve. I'm going to petition the courts to be allowed not to help you. You just threatened me." Samuel was confused and told him that. "You're confused about threatening me? Or simply confused about all of this? Either way, I'm not going to give you what I can simply because you said those things to me. I knew this was going to be wrong as soon as I read over the report. Goodbye, sir."

Before he could ask about who else was going to be coming back, he was shuffled out of the room and to his cell in a matter of minutes. There was no conversation from the cops that took him back, nor would they let him use the phone. Damn it all to hell, somebody better be explaining to him what was going on or he was going to be pissed off. Again.

Things were off in his cell, too. Like his bed wasn't made up, but it looked like someone had started to make his bed. There was fresh toilet paper on the stand where his commode was, and on the little table that he had, there was some paper. Of course, no pencil or pen, but he by god had paper if he wanted to fly an airplane. He started banging on the cell bars to get someone to tell him what was going on.

"What the heck do you want?" The officer seemed to have appeared out of nowhere, and it startled him a bit. "You stop that noise or I'm going to take away your extras."

"What extras? I got nothing in here to write with. The toilet paper isn't the good stuff like my wife used to buy. Hell, I can see right through it." Ignoring what he'd said, the man told him that he had shower privileges in ten minutes. "Well, where is that? And what sort of clothes am I going to be putting on? This orange thing is smelly."

"It's smelly because you are. When was the last time you took a bath or a shower?" He told him that he didn't like getting wet all over, he just did a whores bath. "I have no idea what that means. Get yourself cleaned up or we're going to take you out back and scrub you down with the hose."

"A whores bath? As many times as you've arrested women of the night, and you don't...it's them washing their delicate parts between customers. Christ, I can't believe I have to tell you that. What the hell are you doing here if you're not arresting whores? Why, just the other day I had me one and she cleaned herself right up with one of them moist towels things you get in a bag. Christ, ole mighty, you're dumber than a rock."

"You're to get yourself cleaned up all over your body and hair. You have five minutes to get ready." He didn't like to be rushed into anything, so he told him that. "It's that or the hose, you can take your pick."

He decided that he'd take the shower. He'd been in this jail before, plenty of times, and if they pulled the hose on you, it would tear skin off on account of them using a fire hose to get you clean. Nothing survived that kind of bathing either. No, he was going to take a shower the old-fashioned way.

Chapter 3

Demi was having a blast with the kids. They were good boys, never getting out of line as he kept an eye on them. Today, they were working in his yard picking up sticks that had fallen from the trees in the last storm they'd had. The pile was getting pretty large when he decided that he should have a bonfire with it and cook out some hot dogs with the two of them.

"Aunt Mandy said that we can only have hot dogs once a week. She doesn't like them at all." Demi asked Martin what was wrong that she didn't like them. "She said she saw a show where they showed how they were made, or something like that. She won't eat them, and she doesn't like to cook them for us. It's all right, you know, Mr. Demi. We like all kinds of other food she cooks for us."

"Is she a good cook?" Teddy told him that she was really good when she had a recipe to follow. "I can cook anything with or without a cookbook, but I've had practice on cooking. I love it. She'll get better at it, I'm sure."

"She made us a roast the other day. Used the

crock pot and everything. The house smelled so good. But she had to work late, and we ate at Locke's house that night. I think she put it in the freezer for another night." Teddy got closer to him and whispered the last part. "I think we hurt her feelings about it. She'd worked really hard making it, and we had hamburgers instead that night."

"Yeah, Aunt Mandy cries a lot." Demi asked Martin why they thought she was crying. "I don't know, but she tries really hard in not doing it where we can hear her, like in her room and in the bathroom. We can hear her, though, and it hurts my heart to hear her. Somebody on the phone keeps calling, and she sometimes doesn't answer the phone no more."

He'd been picking up the boys every night while Mandy worked. They were either at Locke's home or one of the other married brothers through the week, and he thought that it was working out great for all of them, especially for Mandy. He'd take them back to his house, give them a snack, or they'd go to the Crockery with him and hang out. But he only called her when he had them, telling her where they were. It couldn't be him making her cry, could it? He needed to look into things for her.

After cleaning up the rest of the yard, the three of them decided that it was nearly time for them to get going. They'd been working in his yard so much that it was beginning to look like someone cared that lived there. Putting the bags of leaves at the end of the road for trash pick-up, he was ready for them to go home. He only had a few days left on his 'vacation' from work, and he'd been making every second of it count.

He'd been sleeping better since that first night. And now that he was getting out of the house early enough in the morning to get things done, he felt better about himself and what he was doing. Yesterday, he'd spent the entire day sorting through his clothing to get rid of the things that were worn out, he no longer wore, or simply didn't like. He had purged two large trash bags full of things that were out at the curb, too. Demi was going to have to pay extra if he kept this up with tossing things out.

Also, he'd been ordering things to fill out his home. There were now bunk beds in one of the extra bedrooms for the boys should they want to spend the night. He had purchased a kitchen table over what he'd had before. It had been a large wire spool that he'd been using, and he was sort of ashamed of himself for thinking that it would be all right to use. Then there were his linens.

The towels that he was currently using had been a housewarming gift from Martha. Ten years ago. They were so worn in places that he could see through them. Some of them were tattered so badly they couldn't even be used for rags, they were in such horrible shape. While he didn't know a great deal about towels, he knew that he wanted them large and cotton. Getting someplace to order them had been his next obstacle he had to jump through. Where did you go to find towels that he liked? Not online. He wanted to be able to touch them before buying them.

It was nearly six when he was on his way to taking the boys home. Since they never knocked, it was their home, Demi would walk into the house behind them and then leave soon after. For the most part, he and Mandy rarely spoke. Which he supposed was all right. They weren't dating or anything, so it was fine by him.

"She's crying. In the kitchen." He asked the boys to go to their room and he'd see what the problem was. "Okay, but don't hurt her, Mr. Demi. She seems like she's going to break to me."

Going to the kitchen, she was wiping her face with a paper towel. He could tell she'd been crying as her nose was red and her cheeks were too. When she noticed him, she smiled, but it didn't reach her eyes. Asking her what was wrong, she acted like there was nothing and told him she'd only just got home from work.

"You've been crying. And the boys told me that you cry when you think they can't hear you." She told him that she'd talk to them about gossiping. "It's not gossip when it's true. What's going on? Who's been calling you?"

"I guess it's right for me to assume that they also told you that I don't always answer the phone, too." He nodded. "I'm fine. Really. I've just been working some overtime at the office and it's catching —" her cell phone rang and she nearly jumped. Instead of answering it, she put it on the counter, telling him she'd get it later. Demi picked it up on the third ring and answered without saying anything.

"Bitch. You'll be turning them kids over to me when I get there. It don't matter to me if you want to or not. I'm not fucking with you." He looked at Mandy when she said his name. "I don't want you to get too comfy with their money either. Don't think that I don't know you're getting a check every month to care for them. I'm going to be taking them home and getting me some of that government money, too."

"Who is this?" She didn't answer him. "Why are you calling this woman who has devoted her love and time to those little boys?"

"She ain't got nothing on me. I should have had them. It's my brother that sired them." Demi told her that Mandy's sister carried them and gave birth to them. "This ain't no contest, dumbass. I should have had them when I was told about their mother being dead. Sammy wants me to have them."

"I remember now why you didn't get them. You couldn't pass the background test. Something about you having a long record of arrests. Yes, I remember that now. You have committed fraud, breaking and entering...to many things for me to—"

"That's got nothing to do with me raising them boys. And the fact that they get a check every month goes a long way for me to want them. How much does she get?" He told her that it wasn't any of her business. "We'll just see about that, won't we? I'm almost there, and when I get there, I expect them to be ready to go back home with me." Then she hung up.

Demi had already broken one phone, so he gently put hers back on the counter. Having her sit down, he got her a glass of water and set it in front of her. Sitting in the other chair, he waited for her to explain, but all she did was stare off into the room.

"How long has she been calling here?" She told him since they'd moved in. "We'll get your phone number changed in the morning. Do you know how she got your number? I'm assuming that Samuel gave it to her when she called him. Isn't she his sister or something?"

"Yes, sister. And I never thought of Samuel giving it to her. She never said, and since he's in jail, it just never occurred to me that he'd ever had it." She looked at him now. "Why are you here?"

"I was dropping off the boys when they told me that you were crying. I came to see what was going on." She nodded and got up to go to the sink. Dumping out the water he'd given her, she poured them both a glass of tea, then put some ice in the glass. "Why didn't you tell one of us you were being threatened?" She put the tea away and handed him one of the glasses before sitting down again.

"Why would I think that you'd care about me and Georgie? She's not related to you. I'm not either. You care for the boys, however, but I want you to know that I'm going to make sure that she can't get them. I've been reading how to go about that on the internet." He snorted at her and he could see that pissed her off. "I'm not stupid, you know. I know that I have to put out a restraining order against her. I'm not sure how to go about it, but I'm learning."

"In the meantime, what will you do if she comes here with a gun? Then demands you hand them over?" Mandy told him she didn't know yet but was working on it. "I'm going to help you. I don't want anything to happen to you or those boys. You've done a good job of keeping them safe, but this might well be over my head as well."

"She said that if she has to, she's going to kill me to get them. For the money, Demi. Not because she wants them around. Why would someone take children out of a good environment and put them into a dangerous situation? Because we both know that's what it's going to be." Demi pulled her into his arms and held her while she cried. It tore at him in ways that it never had before, to have a woman crying about something. "I'll be just fine. You and your family have done enough for me and the boys. I'll take care of it."

"Bull shit." He heard a sharp intake of breath and turned to find the boys in the room with them. "How about you guys get cleaned up, and we'll head to my brother's house. We need to figure out what's going on here."

"Is Aunt Mandy going to be all right? She looks all pinched up again." Demi looked down at the beautiful woman in his arms. "You didn't make her pinched, did you, Mr. Demi?"

"Not this time. Come on. We'll head to my brother's house when you're finished getting cleaned up, and I'll order us some pizza or something." The kids sounded like that was a good idea. He didn't know if it was the drive to his brothers or pizza yet, but he was willing to bet it was the food. What kid didn't like pizza? He turned to Mandy again. "Come on. We'll put our heads together and figure this out. There is no point in you taking this on without help. Between the dozen or so of us, we should be able to figure out a way to keep you guys safe. Because I don't trust her any more than I do her brother."

After calling his brothers and telling them what was going on, they decided that meeting at a pizza place would be faster. Taking the kids to Adornetto's was going to be fun, but the conversation was going to be hard. But he felt like they should know, too, as they had to keep an eye on for themselves. This Georgie person barked up the wrong tree when she messed with his family.

They were the first to arrive and asked to be seated in the middle of the place. It was the biggest table they had, and it just so happened to be close to the kitchens. He ordered ten pizzas, hoping that would be enough to start with, and he also ordered enough salads for the table. He'd take home what they didn't eat tonight.

Bringing out large pitchers of soda and teas when everyone arrived in groups made it so that they could get their drinks poured without having to wait. He was glad when the boys asked for milk with their pizza, and the two of them shared a salad again. He loved these kids.

After Mandy told them everything that had been going on, he put in his two cents about how she had threatened Mandy too. His brothers looked angry, but it was the women that he was the most afraid of.

They looked like they could have called on the U.S. Army to get this woman taken care of, and to be honest, he wasn't sure that they might not try that. Especially Shipley.

"Do you know where she lives? Or if she really is coming here?" She said that she thought that she lived in Kentucky, but she didn't know if she was really coming or not. But she couldn't discount the fact that she knew just where she lived. "Did she say she did? Or maybe suggested that she knew where you lived?"

"She gave me my address and how long I've been living there. I'm fearful that somehow Samuel is telling her things that will cause me more trouble. I just don't know what to do. I know that I can't do this on my own, whatever she has planned, but I also know that you guys have no reason whatsoever to keep me safe."

"You're our friend. And you work for us. Of course, we're going to help you." Demi thought that sounded lame, but he didn't tell Shipley that. "Besides, it's been a good long time since we've had to kick some ass."

It was suggested by Locke that she stay with him for the next few days. But he said that he had more room and said that he'd be able to keep an eye on them at his house. Besides, he told them that he had a gated driveway as well as a fenced-in yard. It would be more difficult for anyone to get past those barriers since they were already in place.

"I do have a place to stay, you know. And a back yard." Demi didn't want to piss her off so he asked her if she'd seen his home. "No. Why would I have? No, we'll stay at home and keep a better eye out for her."

"I would rather you didn't, Mandy." Shipley laid her gun on the table after looking around. "I'm armed all the time, as is Locke and Jack. Even being in this small town can be dangerous. What would you do if she were to come into your home with her own weapon? I'm sorry to say that it would be over before it started. She's already said that she's not above killing you for them. Yes, I know you don't know if that's true or not, but think of how Samuel killed his wife. She'd been used to his beatings, and it got her killed. Please stay with Demi. We'll all feel better about you being safe."

She looked pinched again. Demi thought that was a good word for someone who looked not quite angry but upset all the same. When she asked the boys what they wanted to do, he was both surprised and impressed. They put their heads together and spoke to each other. When they turned to him after a few minutes, Demi felt proud of them.

"You won't hurt her. You've never hurt us, but we don't know about our aunt." He told them that he'd rather die than to hurt any of them. "All right, then we'll stay, but we want you to make sure that Aunt Mandy gets to work and stuff with you. We don't want her hurt either."

"Deal." They shook on it, and he was glad to see the gun was no longer on the table. Ordering another round of pizzas, he was happy to see that everyone was enjoying themselves, including Mandy.

~*~

Mandy didn't want to stay at Demi's house. She knew that it was the best possible place for her to stay without living with one of the others. Besides, the boys loved the man, and she thought that he was all right. Taking in a deep breath, she let it out slowly before correcting herself. She was in love with Demi.

It had happened so slowly that she didn't know really when it had happened. He didn't really have a great deal to do with her when he came to her house. But he did love the boys. And through them, she'd been able to see a part of him that others hadn't. Demi was a good man.

He never treated her with anything but respect. When he'd been to the house, he was polite and kind. Staying for dinner when invited and even cleaning up after they were finished. The boys would tell her some of the things that he'd teach them. Like how to be nice to someone when they were mean to you. How to open the door to a place and allow older people and women to go in first. Apparently, this had been a fun lesson for them as they got their cheeks pinched on occasion and told what wonderful little men they were. They were learning lessons that their own father should have been teaching them, but didn't get, not from Samuel.

The man was a monster. She had night terrors where she would wake up nearly screaming, seeing him beating poor Besty to death. Threatening her and his own children with the next beating. The way he stood over his own wife, her sister, and had beaten her with the ball bat that only that afternoon they'd been playing with in the yard. Who knew that something so innocent, like a child's toy, could be used for such violence.

Shivering, she put the last of her clothing in the closet before closing the doors. She was putting her things in the dresser when Teddy came to see her. He got up on her bed and watched her for several minutes before speaking.

"Mr. Demi told us to call him just plain Demi. Is that all right?" She said it was all right with her so long as he was fine by it. "Okay. Also, he said not to tell anyone that we've moved into his house. He said that he'd make sure that everyone in town knew it too. Do you think that my dad is the one that got that woman to say she was going to kill you? I don't want you to die, Aunt Mandy. You're all me and Martin got in the world."

"I don't want to die either." Getting on the bed with him, she wrapped her arms around him and told him everything that they'd been doing to keep them safe. "So you see, we're taking this very seriously, and you should too. I don't know Georgie, do you?"

"She came around a few times when momma was alive. She locked us up in the closet and beat on momma, too. Something about welfare money. Momma didn't have it on account of Dad taking it already. He was forever making it so that we didn't have any food at the end of the month. She'd have fixings and stuff, she said to us, but nothing like milk and eggs. I tried not to eat so much of them, but momma told me that she'd get us what we needed, some way. I don't know how she did it, but we'd have milk and eggs then. Do you suppose she was stealing them?"

"She'd call me, and I'd send her some money. She might well have stolen them for you boys had I not been able to send her something." She thought of how many times she'd had to help her sister get through the month. "Your mom could stretch a dollar out until it screamed is what our daddy said about her. She was a good mom."

"She was the best." She held him for a bit longer before Martin came into the room, too. He, too, got up on the bed and snuggled with them. It had become a habit, the three of them snuggling nightly. Mandy thought it was to have a good night's sleep, but she needed it as much as they did. Oh, how she loved these little boys.

They'd been living with Demi for the past two days now. It was quiet here, and there were no neighboring kids in the yard. Teddy and Martin would play in the back, but she knew they were nervous about it. After having her number changed on her cell phone, she didn't get any more calls either. The peace and quiet of the phone was the best. After getting the boys up and going, she went to the kitchen to figure out what to have for dinner. She was almost too nervous to cook in Demi's kitchen as he'd gone back to work today in his own restaurant.

"He's going to bring stuff home." She asked Martin how he knew that. "He left you and us a note. Here you go." The note was crumbled and faded, like it had gotten wet at some point.

"Next time, just leave it on the table for me to read, all right?" The grin they gave her made her heart swell up. "What else do you know about our eating arrangements? Is he going to bring home enough for us all to eat, or just him?"

"All of us. He said he's going to make it so that our taste buds have a good education. I don't know about all that. I think my buds are just fine." Teddy laughed with his brother. "Oh yeah, I forgot to tell you too that Ms. Jack is going to come by and see you sometime tomorrow. She came to see us when we were in the back yard. We didn't do anything wrong, she just wants to see you for a little bit. Jack's not a girl's name, is it, Aunt Mandy?"

"Her name is Jacklynn. Someone at some point shortened it for her. Shipley, in the event you were going to ask, is Candance. But since she's been in the service, the army for so long, that's what she goes by." She was distracted trying to understand what parts of the note said. Something about wine and nuts, but she didn't get it. Thinking about calling him to figure it out, she picked up the phone and hoped she wasn't calling at a terrible time. "You guys play in the living room so that I can call Demi to find out what this says. All right?"

They went into the living room. Really, it wasn't much more than a room with sleeping bags and a big television. But they knew how to use the remotes and get to whatever they wanted to watch. She could get it to turn on, but nothing more. Whatever was on, that's what she watched. Someone answered on the first ring.

"May I speak to Mr. Erickson? This is Mandy—" That was as far as she got before she was told to hold on. The next time it was picked up, it was Demi. He wanted to know if she and the boys were all right. "Yes, I just…you left a note, and since it got wet from the boys, I didn't want to mess up something that you said to me. This isn't a bad time, is it?"

"Not at all. I wondered if you were allergic to nuts or any kind of wine. I'm bringing dinner home with me, and thought that I'd ask first if there were any allergies that you three had." She told him none that she was aware of, but she'd ask the kids. After getting an all-clear from them, she told Demi. "All right. I'm training a cook today. I find that after having that week off, I don't want to be here as much as I used to be. I enjoyed hanging out with the three of you."

She didn't know what to think about that, so she didn't say anything. Mandy knew he could well afford not having to work. However, what would that do for them staying with him? After getting off the phone with him, it rang again. While not sure she should answer it, she left it to go to voicemail. He was the only person she knew who had a landline that wasn't business-related. She was surprised to hear Locke's voice telling her to pick up.

"I'm glad that I caught you. Samuel wants to see you. I have a feeling that they've figured out that the phone number you have is no longer working. Also, no one in town or at the jail is going to be giving him any more information. That's how he got your phone number, by the way, not to mention your home address." She asked if she could count on that happening again. "No. The officers have all been told that if they tell him anything at all, they'll be fired. And put in jail. I guess this man who had leaked the information was a friend of Samuels and didn't think it was doing any harm in him telling him tidbits while he was giving him his meals."

"That's good to know, I guess. I'd rather they not have anything to do with him at all, but I don't know what will happen with him." She sat down at the table. "You said Samuel wants to see me. Should I go? I mean, do I trust him enough to go there and be in the same place with him? I'm terrified of him if you want the truth."

"Shipley is going with you, if you don't mind. She's going to keep an eye on you and help you with questions he might have. Sometimes it's better to have a second person there when you get overwhelmed. I know that I've been taking my wife places with me so that I can ask her questions about what was said. She'll be there as your support." Mandy asked when Shipley was ready to go. "I believe she's on her way to see you now. Just get it over with is my motto. That way, you're not worrying needlessly about what's going to happen once you get there."

"You're right, I would worry." She wanted to

ask if Demi could take her, but arrangements had been made, and she'd go with the flow. Besides, he might not want to go with her, so it would be embarrassing for her to ask him. "The doorbell is going off now, so that's more than likely her. One of us will get back to you once I leave. I'm nervous, but I think this is a good thing."

Shipley and Dusty were at the front door, and she was dressed in much the same manner as she was. Jeans and a T-shirt. Pulling on her shoes, some old boots that she'd forgotten about, Dusty was going to stay with the boys. These people were making sure that she was well taken care of, even when she didn't understand that she needed it. Going out of the front of the house, she slipped into her car just as the boys waved at her from the front porch. A good omen, she thought in ways of sending her off to see their father. Christ, she must be insane to do this, but with Shipley around, she did feel marginally better.

Chapter 4

Georgie was pissed off. The phone number she had for the bitch was disconnected. She never would have thought she'd do something like that as she'd been calling her several times a day for nearly a month. Georgie thought that the woman was stupid for even answering her calls in the first place. After about a week of it, hell, a couple of days, she would have changed out her number then.

Samuel hadn't been able to get her new number either. His buddies at the police station weren't giving him shit anymore. Some bigwig had put the hammer down on him getting information. They were his kids by god, why didn't he deserve to have someone checking up on them all the time? Georgie was still about four hours away from his brother and that Mandy person. She'd better be right at the house too, or there was going to be hell to pay.

She and Samuel were twins. They weren't identical, she had to tell people, on account of her having black hair and him having red. She was also taller than him. But other than that, she supposed she could see where people would be confused. They were forever asking them if they were identical. Stupid people.

Georgie was smarter than her brother, too. He might be meaner than her, but that is where her smarts would come in. While she might well have killed Besty—stupid name if you asked her—but she'd been better at it in not getting caught. Like she would have killed her in her bed, not out in the kitchen where anyone could see them. Then she'd run off like she'd not been home. Stuff like he'd done would get you in prison.

Samuel also had tried to kill his sons. Nah, doing that would get you hate from everyone in the prison. Killing kids was a big fat no-no as far as she knew. While not being in prison like her brother had been, she'd been in a lot of jails lots of times. That's where she got all her information about things like her brother was in right now.

In addition to killing Besty, he'd been caught wanting to kill the kids. Then there was the witnesses too. Not just the kids, if she were to beat them enough, they'd not say a word, but the aunt had been there too. Georgie had full intentions of getting her out of the way too. Without her testimony, there wasn't going to be anything they could hold him on. They'd have to let him go. No witness, no prison. Everyone knew that.

Of course, she didn't know about the police and what they'd seen. But she also knew that blackmail would get them to change their mind. Money, too, but she didn't have much of that, so she was going to have to dig deep into their lives to figure out what they'd done before becoming a model citizen. Everyone had something in their past that she could get. And if they didn't, then she'd make things up. She wasn't above doing anything for her brother.

Getting off the highway to get some gas and something to eat, she pulled up to the gas line and waited her turn. She loved how people would look at her truck. It was so jacked up that if she wanted to, she could run right up and over the little cars in front of her if she'd had a mind to. As it was now, she could look down on anyone in line.

Her truck was shiny black with thirty-five-inch wheels and a lift suspension system that raised the body up about four feet, making her a god to the driving world. There were flood lights along the top of the front window, a special light in the roof that turned when she needed it to.

Gunning her engine a little, she was happy to see a couple in their tiny little car get finished up faster and on their way. Pulling to the fueling station, Georgie pulled out her little ladder and made her way down the steps. Yes, sir, she thought, she was a scary bitch when it came to her truck.

Of course, it had cost her everything she'd ever made, too. The lift kit alone had been nearly five grand. The tires were about twenty-five hundred a piece for five of them. Then there was the paint job. Christ, it was no small wonder that she had to sleep in her baby. She didn't have money for anything else after getting it the way she wanted.

After getting gas and paying, Georgie picked up some chips and a six-pack of beer. It was the snack of champions, she told herself. And when she got out to her baby, she opened up the chips — nothing but spicy hot ones for her, she opened up a can of beer for the road. The entire six-pack wouldn't be enough to get her drunk, but it was enough to give her a buzz. And that was all she wanted to have to deal with Mandy and the kids.

Georgie was on her way a few minutes after drinking her second beer and downing nearly half the bag of chips. Burping loudly, she pulled into traffic just as her cell phone rang. Looking at the face that came up, she was glad that she'd put the number in for her brother on his contact list the last time he'd been in jail. Saved her time in trying to figure out who was bothering her all the time.

"Speak." Smiling, she knew that it would throw him off when she didn't say hello. Just as she figured, he asked her to stop screaming in the phone and answer correctly. "Then don't call me anymore if that's the way that you feel. Whatcha want anyway?"

"I can't get nothing from nobody around here. They're all about as close-mouthed as I've ever seen. You almost here?" She told him that she only had about four hours to go. "Good. You come to the jailhouse when you get here. I've asked for Mandy to come and see me. I'm going to see if I can butter her biscuits to get some information from her. Maybe she'll bring the kids with her. I hope so. I need to know what they been saying about me and shit."

"If anything happens to you and you don't get out right away, can you give me permission to live in that government house while I gots them? Might be better than all three of us living in my truck. Besides, I'd like to have a place to keep my beers cold. You need anything?" Her brother said he'd like to have a couple of beers himself; he was going through some terrible shakes. "I'll grease a few palms to get you a couple in. You still drinking that cheap shit? You know that I won't join you when we're talking if you are. That shit is nasty. I'll get us something to munch on, too, while we converse."

She thought about the house that her brother had been living in with Besty. It had three big bedrooms and a nice-sized kitchen. She didn't cook, that shit was for the birds but she could stock up a fridge really good with things that she liked. Then she thought of the kids.

"What do kids eat? I've never been around them much, you know?" He said they just ate regular food, like people ate. "I don't know what that will mean. I tell you what, I'll just play it by ear to see how much shit they'll eat. But I draw the line at feeding them steaks and shit. You said there was a food card for them, didn't you? I can get me some steaks and taters. I'll love that."

"They eat cereal too. I don't buy it, of course, Betsy did the shopping, but I've seen them eat it. Hot dogs and pizza, too. They eat that crap up." She asked about drinks. "I don't know, Georgie. Just buy some water or give them some out of the sink. Christ, I didn't hang around them all that much. They're kids. Just tell them that they're eating what you give them, and that's the end of it."

"All right, cool you engines. I can figure it out on my own. But I need you to tell someone that I'm going to be living in that house of yours. I have me some plans. Anyway, I'm going to go to that Mandy's place in the morning, first thing. Well, when I get up. It might be later in the afternoon. I'm needing me some downtime before I'm around those kids. Another question I have for you. Are they brats? Am I going to have to show them who their boss is? I don't mind that, I'm thinking I might enjoy it a bit, but you tell me what kind of brats they are." Again, he told her that he didn't know. "How can you be their daddy if you don't know them at least a little bit? Damn it, Samuel, how am I supposed to be prepared for them? I don't have a belt or anything to use on them. I guess I could use a switch, but that ain't going to be the same thing. You remember how Daddy and Momma would beat us? The belt with a big buckle was the worst."

"Yeah, I remember. I don't think that Besty beat them at all, and you know that aunt of theirs is going to be the same way. Good Christ, it's going to be hard to be around them all the time, I can tell you that." Georgie asked if they had a back yard. "Yeah, there is one. A nice big one, but don't put them there with a bowl of water and some crackers. I guess that's against some kind of abuse rule you can't do. I don't understand why that's a rule, they're my fucking kids."

"I'm not going to be asking permission to do anything to them, just so you know. If I have to be around them all the time, they're going to do what I tell them, and that's final." She thought her brother said good luck with that, but wasn't going to get into an argument with him. "I'm going to have to get off here if I'm going to have any minutes left before I get that money card from the government. I'm looking forward to having some cash on me all the time."

"Don't be spending it all up the first day. I mean, with me being in here, I won't be able to get with my guy about buying out the rest of the food one for cash. And that shit comes in handy too." She said she'd pace herself. "You'd better if you know what's good for you. And take me some pictures, too, you can show me next time you come in. I wanna see what you do to Mandy about her taking my kids."

She didn't bother telling him yes or no. Her minutes were ticking down, and until she got to the house and got those cards, she was going to be in trouble. It was bad enough that she'd had to steal a card to come this far. Buying money for a phone card would alert the cashier that it wasn't hers. She couldn't figure out how long they'd been putting faces on the cards. Just getting the beer and chips had been scary, in getting caught.

It was nearly midnight when she pulled into the drive where her brother had lived. There was a large dumpster out front of it, but she didn't pay it any mind. Instead, she got out her sleeping bag, laid it across the seats, and laid down. She'd get in tomorrow at least, but for now, she needed a little nap. Then she remembered that she was supposed to see Samuel. Getting up, she headed there now. Stupid fuckers, making it so she had to inconvenience herself to go to the jail to see him. It shouldn't be a crime to her way of thinking to beat around your spouse. Okay, she told herself she'd killed her spouse, but like before, she'd make it so there were no witnesses.

They wouldn't allow her to see him. It was too late, they told her, and Samuel hadn't been a good boy today, so he'd lost his privileges of having company unless she was his attorney. Going back out to her truck, she was so pissed off that she wanted to run over every cruiser in the lot. She didn't, of course, they'd catch her, but she was sorely tempted.

Going by the Dari Mart on her way back to the house, she picked her up some brews and hoped to Christ nobody said anything to her or they'd be picking up pieces of the person for a long time. She was just pissed enough to ram her little baby right up the ass of the place if they were to give her any shit about the card.

Getting back to the house, she looked in the dumpster to see if there was anything she could use. Since it was empty, she figured that someone was going to be doing some house cleaning. There was still yellow tape around the house, but she wasn't concerned about that. Whatever mess was still in her house when she moved in, she'd make the brats clean it up. That's about all they were good for, she knew.

It was just going on one in the morning when she

was settling down in her makeshift bed. Tomorrow, she'd have a real bed under her and a shower, too, if she was inclined. While she didn't know where she was going to pick up the cards from, she was going to make that a priority. Georgie had a fridge to fill up and she wasn't going to waste any time in fucking around with people to get it, damn it.

Someone pounding on her window woke her up. Sitting up, burping some of the beer she'd drank last night she finally got out of the truck and asked the man what the fuck he wanted. He told her that she couldn't park here.

"I'm going to be living here soon. My brother has this place." Wiping the snot out of her eyes, she went to where the driveway ended and blew out the snot from her nose too. "He's got himself nice digs, but I'm going to be moving into them until he gets himself out of jail."

"You're disgusting. And we've been told that the woman who lived here is gone, and her kids are with their aunt. You'll need to move on." She tried to tell him again that she was the owner of the place, but he told her that he'd have to call the police if she didn't move on right now. "If you want to talk to someone about living here, you'll have to go through the proper channels. I don't know what they are. But we've been contracted to clean this place out as the family has gotten everything they want from here."

"I'm going to be living here with that stuff. You just hold your horses. I'm gonna need that stuff with the kids." He told her again to take it up with the proper channels. "I don't have me a television, you idiot. What channel am I supposed to be watching?"

He just stared at her and walked away. She hated it when people did that. Damn it, she wanted answers. Getting back in the truck, she was tempted again to run some of the workers down, but she didn't. Instead, she headed to the police station again to get in and see her brother. He'd better have some answers for her.

The station house was busy when she got there. Telling the man at the main desk she wanted to see her brother, they had to pat her down, they told her. So much for her sneaking Samuel in a beer, she thought when they took it from her. The chips didn't get to go back with her either, as they'd been opened. Nobody could tell her why that was an issue. They'd just have to open them when she got back there. She hated people.

~*~

"She pulled into town about midnight and went to stay at the house where Besty lived." Mandy asked where she was now. "You can't miss her truck; it's the biggest thing you've ever seen. Wherever it is, she's there. But in answer to your question, she's at the stationhouse with her brother."

She'd been stopping off at one of the little shops in town to delay her going to see her brother. Glad for the network that the little town had going, she knew now that she didn't want to go and see either of them. However, Shipley thought it was the perfect time to go and talk to them both at the same time. So here she was making her way to the stationhouse to see not just the man who killed her sister, but the woman who wanted to kill her to take the boys from her.

"Just tell them what you've been practicing. And remember, I'm with you as a witness." She asked her why she thought that she needed a witness. "You always need a witness when idiots are concerned. They're called idiots for a reason. Being in the service, I've been around the worst of them."

She was taken back to his cell, where he was talking to Georgie. Letting the two of them get a good look at her, she had to tell them who she was. Samuel said that she was lying about who she was, and Georgie told her that she was a lot prettier than she remembered.

"Since I've never met you before, I don't know how that would be an issue. I've come to tell you both that I'm not going to be threatened or hurt by either of you, or I'll press charges against the two of you." Georgie stood up from her chair and sat back down when Shipley put her hand on her gun. She was happy now that she'd brought her. Samuel asked her what her new phone number was. "I'm not going to give that to either of you. I like my quiet and not being bothered by the two of you. Also, you should know that I'm going to adopt Teddy and Martin."

"Who's that?" She then had to explain that they were the kids that he'd sired. "Well, why didn't you say that in the first place. Damned kids. I knew I should have been around when she popped them out. I surely wouldn't have named them that."

"Be that as it may, they're going to be mine in a few weeks, and there will be nothing you can do about it." Georgie laughed and said they'd see about that. She might not want to get used to breathing when she came around. "Breathing? You mean you're going to do something to me that keeps me from breathing?"

"You bet your sweet ass I am. I'm going to do to you what Samuel did to your sister. Beat the daylights out of you so I won't be bothered by you." She asked her why she'd want to kill her. "Because you're in the way of me getting those kids and the shit that comes with raising them. I don't know shit about them but you can bet that I'm going to be using their benefits all up. Then we'll see if they live long enough for their daddy to get out of jail. They might get themselves dead before too much longer."

"You know they record what is being said back here." Georgie looked up at the camera that was pointed right at her and pointed her fingers at it like a gun and made a noise that she supposed was like a gunshot. "What is that supposed to mean? You think you'll get a gun back here? You couldn't even get a beer back here with some chips. What makes you think that a gun is going to be any easier?"

"I got my ways. You'd be surprised at how resourceful I am. Especially when it comes to family. Nah, you don't have to worry your little head about cameras catching me. I'm above that." Rolling her eyes, she realized that they really were idiots. "You'll be waiting on me to come and get the kids, too. Nobody is going to be standing there holding a gun on me when I come for you, either."

"Come on, Mandy, it's time we left." Nodding, the two of them backed themselves down the long hall back to the door. Once they were both on the other side of it, she looked in the window and saw that Georgie hadn't moved, but that didn't make her feel any safer. "You have to press charges against Georgie. All right? She threatened you and the boys. They'll be able to hear it when they go over the recordings. Come on now, you're all right. Just tell them what she said to you."

"She really would kill me." Shipley said she'd

never get the chance. "You can't be with me twenty-four seven. I have to go to work and take care of the boys."

"You'd be surprised too with what we can do to keep you safe. I'm going to make a few phone calls and get us some help. That woman is worse than her brother. She'd kill someone for anything she deems against her. We'll take care of her. You'll see."

She didn't want anyone getting hurt protecting her. The boys, yes, but not her. Telling Shipley that they were standing in front of the captain when she nearly broke down. She might well die from just taking care of two little boys who meant the world to her.

"You have to protect the boys at all costs." Shipley said that they'd do the same for her. "No, I want your promise that you'll make sure that Teddy and Martin are your first priority. I promised Besty a long time ago to make sure they grew up to be fine men if she were to die, and I'm asking you for the same promise. Please? They have a life to live without fear of being killed."

"I can't make that promise, Mandy. You've come to mean a great deal to us, and I won't allow her to take you from us." She nodded and told her that she'd just ask Demi to do it. "I don't think that you're going to get any of us to make that kind of promise to you. Like I said, you've come to mean a great deal to us and the boys."

After pressing charges against Georgie, she felt better knowing that she was going to be in a jail cell next to her brother. The courts didn't have a judge all the time, so they'd only have until he came around again to hold her. Hopefully, she'd be in her cell as long as her brother was. Forever.

By the time she was in the car, she was shaking. Her entire body felt like she'd been run over a couple of times, then put out on the line to dry. Shivering, Shipley wrapped her up in a blanket and then drove. She didn't care where they were going so long as it wasn't home. The boys were there, and they'd ask questions she didn't have an answer to.

When they pulled up in front of The Crockery Pot, she was never so glad to see Demi standing out there waiting for her in her life. As soon as she was in his arms, she broke down. It was talk to him or she'd be driving herself crazy trying to keep it all in. Babbling now, she told him what had been done to her this morning.

"I have you." Nodding while he dragged her into the restaurant. "Come on now, I've got you. I have some things to tell you, too, about the Jameson people. They think that just because she's come all this way to get the kids, she's entitled to the money that Besty was getting. Not to mention the house and card that was used for gas for transportation."

"How did you find that out?" He told her how Georgie had gone to the house last night and parked in the driveway. "So she wants the boys because of the money that he can get. I'm supposed to get a check each month for caring for them, but I was going to put that in the bank for them to use for college. It's really not all that much. I think I was told that it would be twenty-five hundred a month."

"Per child. And yes, you'll get that. Zander is setting up things for you to get a food card and also money to get you a car. You might not need it, but it's coming for the boys." She nodded, thinking that whatever it was, she'd use it just on them. "Maybe you can get them some hot dogs once in a while."

"I will not." Demi laughed, and she smiled at him. "I can't stand them. Hot dogs, I mean. When they want them as a dinner, I usually treat myself to a quart of ice cream to compensate for having to cook them. Gross."

"I know you give in to them more than once a month, too. Teddy told me that you've even made them chili to go with them. You're a good aunt to them." She thanked him and then looked at him. Really looked hard at him. "What? Do I have spinach in my teeth? I've been trying some of the things that the new cook is making. You should have some, they're really quite delicious."

"I'm in love with you." She wanted him to say something, but he just stared at her. "I'm sorry if that isn't anything you want to hear, but I thought that if something happened to me, then you'd know."

"I don't know what you expect me to say to that." She said that he didn't have to say anything. "I like you. You're a good mother to the boys, but I'm not looking for someone in my life right now. I have a lot going on and I don't —"

She stood up and smiled at him. It was difficult to make her eyes say what she'd just said to him when her heart was shattered. Telling him that she needed to get home, that the boys would be waiting on her, she left without another word. Glad that he was being called away when she did, Mandy was afraid that she'd say something else to him that would have her in tears if he said anything more than he'd already said. As soon as she was in the car, she broke down in front of Shipley.

"You're in love with him." She nodded, not even able to keep that to herself. "I thought as much when I brought you here. What did he say to you that has you in tears?"

"He likes me all right." She laughed. "I didn't pour my heart out to him, tell him why I've fallen in love with him, but I did tell him that I was in love with him. He'll more than likely want me to move out of his house now."

"No, he'd not do that. He might avoid you more, but he'd also want to keep you safe." Nodding, she asked if they could go home. "Yes, of course. But let's get some lunch first. I'm starving and it's past one now."

"I'm not really hungry. But sure, I'll go with you." When they pulled out into traffic to go to the only other place to eat in town, they ended up at a pizza shop. The two of them were being seated when she thought of something. "Don't tell anyone, please? I'm going to be…it's going to be hard enough to be around him, much less the entire family if they find out. I don't know that I could handle that."

"All right. I don't like it, but I understand. I'm a bit pissed off at Demi but that's all on me." She told Shipley that it wasn't his fault that she'd fallen in love with him. "No. But he could have been nicer about it, other than saying that he liked you all right. That's kind of mean if you ask me."

After ordering a large pizza for the two of them, Shipley eyed the salad bar. Telling her to go for it, the other woman left her sitting there while she filled up a plate of mostly vegetables. Mandy didn't think she could eat anything right now and wasn't surprised when she was given a plate of carrots and dressing to munch on. After a couple of carrots, she did feel better. She looked at Shipley.

"Do you think I should have told him? I mean, my reasoning sounds kind of lame right now. 'If anything happens to me, I wanted you to know.' It sounds stupid when I say it to you. I could have gone my whole life without seeing the panic look in his eyes, you know." She told her that he'd come around to her. "I don't want him to settle with me. I want the passion that I see in your face when you look at Dusty. Or when Locke is asked about his own wife. His settling for me would be worse than having him say he loves me too when I know he doesn't."

"I'm sorry. I truly am." She ate a couple of slices of pizza when it arrived, and she was happy that the subject was changed. Anything would be better than being turned away when you were a love-sick person.

Chapter 5

Demi hated himself. He hated the way he'd spoken to Mandy. He should have been kinder to her with his words. Something that he'd never...she loved him. When did that happen, or even how? He'd not really spent any time with her, and now she was saying that she loved him.

"Are you going to tell me what's wrong? You've been mumbling to yourself for the last ten minutes. Something about Mandy and loving someone else." He looked at his brother Knox. "Well? Spill it or not, but you're here to help me not take your mood out on me."

"She loves me." He told him congratulations. "No, you don't understand. I don't love her. I like her...I told her that I like her all right, but I don't love her. I don't want to love her."

"So don't." Demi told him it wasn't that easy. "Sure, it is. I'm assuming that you told her that you didn't want to love her, and she's all right with that? If she is, then you're off the hook. Go on the way that you are."

"I'm afraid that she's made it awkward now. How am I supposed to be around her when she has this thing for me?" Knox told him that he was reading too much into it. It looked like the two of them were getting along just fine. "But she loves me. How am I supposed to let that go?"

"You don't let it go, but you don't dwell on it either. You're the one who is making it awkward, not her. She's still the same person, and so are you. What has you tied up in knots over this? You're being stupid." He thanked his brother for being so understanding. "I think that you're protesting too much. I think that you really do love her, but you're saying this now because she told you first. That's what I think."

"Now, who's being stupid? I don't love her, moron. I like her, but I don't…don't you think that I'd know if I love her or not? I've seen love on our brothers. I don't feel that mushy around her. Nor do I want to… you're just wrong." He told him that he didn't think that all love was the same. "So the three brothers that have wives, all of them treat them the same way too — but they love their wives and are mushy around them. I mean, there are times when I find them to be slightly sickening. Don't you?"

"No, not at all." Knox sat down in the chair that was across from his desk. "Think about how you feel about her. I mean, don't just say that you like her, tell me what it is that you like about her. I'm assuming that you have something that you find likable about her. What is it?" Demi leaned back in his chair and thought about what he was asking. "Don't think too hard on it, big brother. Just tell me what you like about her."

"She has beautiful eyes. Not only that, but they shine when she's happy. I find myself figuring out something to say to her to make them shine. And when she's deep in thought, you can almost see when she gets something. Understands what it is that she's thinking about." Knox told him to go on. "Her skin is flawless. I mean, if there is a scar or any other blemish there, I've never seen it. It kinda glows, too, when she's out in the sun. Like the sun has kissed her and brought out the freckles dancing across her nose."

"Really? And you don't love her? I think you're more sappy than the others are." He asked what he was talking about. "Dude, you just waxed poetry about her freckles, dancing freckles, I might add. What else are you not in love with her about?"

"I'm not telling you anything more. You're just looking for reasons to think that I'm in love." Knox told him that he really wasn't. "All right. Her laughter is the highlight of my day. No matter too if she's laughing at me or with me, I lo—like it." He thought about the last time he'd heard her laugh. He didn't think he'd heard her since she'd told him that she loved him. Demi looked at his brother when something else occurred to him.

"What? What's happened?" Demi said that he'd really hurt Mandy. "I would say that's true. I don't imagine many women go around telling someone they love them only to be told that you like her all right. Seems like you were sort of cruel to her."

"I didn't mean to be." Knox said that he didn't think that he had. "I don't know what to do about this. I enjoyed our friendship. I enjoy being around her, too."

"Yeah, I got that. Demi, I think that if you really were to think about her and you, you really do love her. You just haven't caught up with her yet. I bet that if you really think hard about her, you'll see that she's perfect for you. I mean, you already love the kids, it's only another step or two before you're madly in love with her too. And it sure would make it easier on her if you did love her in order for her to raise those boys as her own." He asked his brother if he was suggesting that he marry her for the kids. "No. I didn't say that at all. I'm thinking that you're also looking for someone to have a fight with over this. I'm not who you should be talking to. And like I said, you seem to be in love with her already, but that could only be me."

"It is only you. As I've said several times already, I don't love her. She's just a good friend to me." Knox nodded but didn't look convinced. "Go away before we get into a fight. I don't want to knock you around because of a woman."

After Knox left him, Demi worked on the order he'd been going over for the restaurant. His new chef, Margo, had put the order together, and he couldn't find anything wrong with her calculations. Demi was ready to turn it over to her as soon as she had another couple of busy nights under her belt. He was ready to move on.

His computer had gone to sleep when he realized that he'd not been thinking about Margo or the restaurant at all. His mind had been centered wholly on Mandy and the boys. They were, he knew, a package deal, and for some reason that made him feel good about liking her. Because he did. He liked Mandy very much.

They were friends. Just last night, she'd made dinner for the four of them. It was good too. Teddy had said that she could cook all right with a recipe. But nothing on her own. Maybe he'd show her how to cook more creatively. Having them all living with him was going to be hard to let go of when she moved back to her house, he only just realized. He loved having them all around all the time.

Getting up after sending the order on its way, he began putting together some of the things that were going to go into the soup he wanted for the evening.

People loved his odd soups. Like last week, he'd had salad soup. It had been a big hit with the creamy lettuce, bacon, and tomatoes with just a pinch of cheese on it before serving. Then there was the loaded baked potato soup that he'd made a couple of nights ago, served with a couple of slices of crusty bread. It was an easy way to get rid of too many baked potatoes, too. He found himself wondering if Mandy would enjoy it as well.

"Damn it." He couldn't seem to keep his mind on track without thinking about Mandy. He didn't love her, but he was thinking about her a great deal, and that was driving him crazy. "Focus, Demitrius. Focus on what's going on right now."

"Did you say something?" Margo came into the room with him and smiled. "I have to have a good talk with myself, too, sometimes. Especially when it feels like something more is going on. Who is the non-focusing person on your list today?"

"A woman." She nodded and told him they were the worst kinds of people to get out of your head. "I didn't know you were with someone. I thought that you said you weren't married or something along those lines."

"I have a girlfriend. She's cool. We've been seeing each other for about ten years now. So we've been there, done that sort of relationship." He told her congratulations. "Thanks. But if you ever want to talk, I'm here for you. Like I said, we've been through it all from breakups to makeups and everything in between."

They did talk, but nothing about Mandy. He told her about the boys and how much he loved being around them. He did mention that he had a roommate now that there was trouble brewing for her, and how he was protecting her from a brother and sister.

"Mandy Wilson, right? I heard about her and Samuel. Those boys, they're polite as can be when I've seen them out and about. Mandy is doing a good job of keeping them on the straight and narrow, too. You two should hook up. She'd be good for you." He asked her why she'd say that. "I'm only making an observation about the two of you. I see the way you two look at each other. It's very hot."

"I don't look at her like that." She just laughed but didn't say anything more. "I like her just fine, but I don't love her."

"If you say so. But let me ask you this, would it bother you to have her date one of your single brothers? I kind of think that one of them will ask her out if you don't stake your claim soon." For some reason that bothered him. Would she date someone else, loving him the way she said? That would be just...he didn't like that. He caught himself rubbing his heart while thinking of which brother he was going to have to beat up for…he looked at Margo when she said his name.

"You got it bad, don't you? I mean, you're really in love with her. That's wonderful for you both." Was he in love or just jealous of his brothers dating her? Something was seriously wrong with him if he was in love with her. But he didn't know what it was. Looking at Margo, he suddenly wanted to go home and see Mandy. "I've got this if you want to go. And if I run into trouble, which I don't see happening, I know how to call you."

"Thanks." He grabbed his shirt and was pulling off his smock as he was going out the door, nearly running Mandy down when she was just opening the door to the back of the restaurant. "I'm sorry. Are you all right?"

"Yes. I was just coming to ask you if you'd watch over the boys tonight. I have plans." He asked her what her plans were, a little too harshly he realized when she looked at him with a cocked brow. "Knox asked me to go to dinner with him tonight. He said he was tired of being hit on when—"

"No. I forbid it." She took a step back, her smile wavering just a little. "He's too handsy with the women he goes out with, and you're not to go out with him. That's final."

He knew he was messing things up with her,

but he couldn't keep his mouth from flapping. Instead of shutting up, he went on to tell her the other things that he knew of his brother and made up a few too. He didn't want her going out with anyone. But him.

"I'll go with him if he wants a date." Mandy laughed, and he didn't care for that either. There was something very badly wrong with him today. "In fact, while under my roof, you'll not date at all. I'm going to be putting my foot down on that. And anything else to do with men that come sniffing around."

The slap to his face stung. Not only that, but he could taste a bit of blood in his mouth from her hitting him. As she turned on her heel and walked away from him, the fool that he'd suddenly become went after her, dragging her around so that she faced him. This time, when she hit him, Demi felt the air whoosh out of him and his head bang against something hard. Then nothing.

When he woke up, Demi tried to sit up, but his brother Locke pushed him back down, telling him to stay put. That was when he noticed that there were medics around him and the bright lights of an ambulance. He asked him what happened.

"Mandy called me to tell me that she had just knocked the shit out of you and that I might want to call an ambulance. So I called them first and then came here. What did you do to piss her off?" He asked him why he thought it was his fault. "Because she's sobbing with my wife right now about you being a neanderthal bastard that thinks he can control her life. So again, little brother, what did you do to have her pop you in the nose with her forehead and walk away?"

"She said she loved me." Locke said that any fool could see that. "Well, I didn't. She told me that she loved me, and I only like her. I think. I don't know what I feel for her now that she's hurt me. Why would you do that to someone you love?"

"Plenty of reasons that I can think of right off the top of my head. She also said that she wasn't to see men while living under your roof. Please tell me you didn't say that to her." Demi said he might well have. "You're an idiot. Why would you say…did you actually tell her that you didn't love her but liked her? Are you insane? Everyone around the two of you can see that you love each other."

He thought about what his brother said to him as the medics were telling him he needed stitches in the back of his head. Didn't sound to him like he was loved. As he was being helped up off the ground, he asked where Mandy was.

"Last I heard, she was moving back into her rental. She said she wasn't going to be living with someone like you, and she thought that she stood a better chance of being normal without you in her life.

You did a number on her, Demi. She's about as pissed off as I've ever seen a woman." He said he wasn't all that happy either. "Yeah, I got that too. But she's crying and you're not. At least not now. You gotta fix this, Demi. She could be your everything."

"I figured that out already. I'm a fool." He said he was only a fool if he didn't fix this with her. "I don't even know how to begin. I've already pissed her off enough that she's moving out of the safeness of my home to someplace a known would be killer knows where she lives."

"I don't know what to tell you. But if she quits working for the women, you're going to have a whole lot of new hurts on your pretty body." He got into the ambulance and was being taken to the hospital when he thought of something else.

The boys were going to be pissed off too when they found out that he'd hurt their aunt. It wouldn't matter to them that he'd been in the hospital; they had told him not to hurt her, and he had. And he felt terrible about it.

By the time he'd gotten to the hospital, his head was hurting, and so was his pride. He'd just, in one afternoon pissed off three of the most wonderful people in the world with his mouth. Once he was able to make a call, he called Mandy to tell her he was sorry.

"Are you all right?" He said that he was but

had a headache. "Good. You deserve it. The things you said to me? I can't believe that I even wanted to speak to you right now. You hurt my heart."

"I don't know why I said those things to you. I'm profoundly sorry. As I said, I don't know why I said those things. I've been thinking about how I feel about you, and I got angry when you said you were going out with my brother. I didn't care for that at all." She told him no shit. "Yeah, well, I'm sorry. Will you come here and sit with me? I just want to talk to you for a little bit. Bring the boys."

"They're unpacking their things. They're not at all happy with me either. We've moved back into our little house. It was that or I murder you in your sleep. To think that I actually told you that I loved you." He asked her if she still did. "Of course. You can't just turn that shit off and on. But I'm pissed off at you for treating me like…I don't know what, but I won't have you treating me that way again."

"I won't. You have my word on that. I was stupid and foolish for even thinking things like I did." She asked him what he was thinking. "That I was going to lose the best thing that has ever happened to me. I think I'm about as deeply in love with you as I've ever been with anyone before."

"I love you too." He wanted to bask in that idea of being in love, but they were taking him to have his head examined. He had a feeling that they were going to need more than an MRI machine to see what was wrong with him.

~*~

Carrie looked at her mom. She'd been doing so much better at the facility than she'd been doing with her at home. Just finding out that she'd been mistreated by the nurse she'd hired hurt her soul, but she was getting the kind of care that she needed now, and so was Carrie.

"Carrie, where are you?" Today was turning out to be a good day for a visit. She mostly knew who she was, and for that, she was grateful. Her mom was in the end stages of Alzheimer's and dementia caused by a stroke that had limited some blood to her brain. "I need to go home and get dinner started, and I can't get out of this chair."

"That's so you don't fall again. See? You busted up your knee the other day when you tried to walk to the lounge." This place had it all. From memory care units to specialized places where her mom could feel comfortable while she was out and about. "Tell me what you had for lunch today? I missed coming to eat with you."

"I don't know. They called it fish, but it looked like a hamburger to me." It had been spaghetti with a slice of garlic toast. "For dessert, I had me a banana.

I've not had one of them in a long time. Put that on the list for when we go shopping again."

The 'banana' hadn't been fruit at all but a slice of cake with pink icing on it. It was one of the other residents' birthday, and the entire ward got to celebrate it with her. Not that she understood any more than her mom did, but it was nice of the staff to make sure every milestone was celebrated. She would be ever so thankful to the Ericksons for what they'd given her in the way of a job and a place to live where her mom was safe.

She'd met the Ericksons when she'd been a grocery store clerk. She'd been ringing out people when one of the men came through her line. Getting him to purchase a winning scratch-off card was easy, and it had come back on her, too. Five grand. And since he'd not needed the money, he'd made sure that she had it. The money was stashed away in an account that her family couldn't get to right now, and she was banking every penny she could while working for them, too.

"When are we leaving here? I need to get home and watch my shows." There was no way that she'd be able to keep her mom safe if she were to leave here, so Carrie changed the subject. Asking her about the dog that came around all the time. "He's so sweet, Carrie. Like he knows that he's loved or something. I want to get me a dog for home. When are we going home today? I need to watch my shows, you know."

"They've been on already, Mom. You and I watched them together." She hated lying to her, but it was easier than telling her that she didn't watch daytime television and that they'd been in the lounge when someone else had them on. "I have to be going soon, Mom. Want me to take you back to the rec center?"

"I want to go home. Damn it, why can't I go home?" She told her that Allen was looking for her. "Oh. He'll hurt me bad, won't he? They all hurt me bad, Carrie. Why would they hurt their poor old mother like that?"

"I wish I knew." While mom couldn't remember faces or times, she remembered how Allen had nearly beaten her to death once. Allen was the worst of her siblings—having five brothers and three sisters had gotten her in trouble with them, too. Allen, being the oldest, she figured that he'd had the most practice at being a cold-hearted monster. He'd beaten her so badly once that she could no longer carry a child, it had been that violent.

They were still out there looking for her because they thought that her checks and Mom's social security checks came to them and damn what Mom might need it for. It had gotten to the point where she was working three jobs just to make it so she could buy Mom's meds when the two of them were living in the house.

Carrie would be grateful for the Ericksons because of what they did for her mom. They paid for her being in a specialized home so that she could work full-time for them. She wrote programs for computers to make them do what it was they wanted. A few weeks ago, she set up an online grocery store ordering app that they were using now to teach women without a job so they could work at home as a domestic worker in some of the finer homes across the county.

She was very careful when she left the nursing home. Terrified that they'd find their mom was a big motivator. Her mom was all she had in this world, and if her family found her, she shuddered to think what they'd do to her. Just to get money. It was always about money with them.

Her apartment was in a secure building. No one got in or out without permission from the people who lived there. Carrie had gone as far as to not putting her name on the button that went with her apartment, so they couldn't just happen on her first name or her last name of Sharp. She didn't want to meet up with any of them as much as her mom didn't. They were dangerous, the lot of them.

By the time she got home, never taking the same way twice, she was glad that she'd put herself something in the crockpot for dinner. She loved soups of all kinds, and when she'd seen her best buddy Demi the other day, he'd given her the fixings for a large pot of the spicy chili so that she could freeze it and have it over the next few months. Carrie loved chili.

She was just settling down with a big bowl when someone pressed the button that was for her to open it. There was a camera on the buttons that had been installed by the Ericksons, and she could see who was there. It was Syble, the oldest girl in her family. Not answering her, she finally looked up at the camera and smiled. It was her fake smile, Carrie knew so well.

"I'm looking for my little sister. I heard that she lived here. Can you let me in so I can check? I've been worried sick over her since I can't find her." She didn't answer her again. "Come on, please? She owes me a great deal of money, and I'm looking to get it back from her. Can you just let me in?"

Picking up her new cell phone, she blindly pushed buttons. When someone answered, she didn't know who, she whispered that she'd been found and that her sister was trying to get into the building. Whoever it was said they'd be there soon and hung up. Whatever happened now was quite literally life or death.

Syble tried her scam on the other people in the building and was told to leave now before they called the police. She wondered at some point if this were to happen, would they sell her out. But apparently, when you had a secure building, people tended to be secure for themselves, too. No one let her in.

"Can I help you?" She knew the voice. It was Knox. He'd been the one that she'd called. And right now, he was talking to her sister. "You're not a resident here. I know everyone who lives here. No one is going to let you in."

"My sister lives here, I think. I saw her the other day coming this way, but her name isn't on the bell thing." He asked her name. "Carrie Sharp. She's been hiding out because she owes me some money. If she's living here, a great deal of money."

"I don't know anyone by that name living here. You need to move on before the police are called." She asked him why he'd just call the police when she wasn't doing anything. "Because you're trespassing. That's against the law. The people here enjoy their privacy, and you're messing with that. Move along or I'll have you moved."

"Damn, I was just looking for my sister. She's not at any of her jobs that she had, and I can't find my mother either. I think she's done something to her. I'm going to file a missing person thing to find her. She owes me money." She was barking up the wrong tree if she thought that any of the Ericksons would fall for that trick. Knox asked how much she owed her. "Are you gonna pay me so I go away? Great. Mom's checks each month are about two grand. I don't know where Carrie is or what she's doing. But if she lives here, then—"

"First of all, I said she didn't live here. I know the residents of this place. I own the building. Secondly, why are you taking your mother's social security check? That's what you're talking about, aren't you? I'm sure that she could use it more than you. You look fit enough to have a job." She asked him if he liked what he saw. "Don't be disgusting. I was talking about you being able-bodied. Get a job and leave your sister and mother alone. I'm sure if they've gone missing, it's because of you. Now, as I said before, move along or I'm calling the police. This residence is for the people who live here."

"You're not nice at all. I'm only asking to get into the building to see if my sister is living here. She could be holed up with one of the people that live here, and you'd never know it." Knox put his arms over his chest. "What are you doing to look like that? Bench pressing trucks? It'll only take five minutes. That's all."

"No." Then he pulled out his cell phone and told Syble that she'd worn out her welcome. To get out of here before he really did call the police. "I'm not kidding right now, I will call them."

"Bastard. I was just asking." Syble turned her

back to him, then turned back. "Carrie, if you're in there, I'm going to find you, and when I do, I'm going to turn you over to Allen. We'll see how happy he is with you when I find you."

Backing away from the camera, she was suddenly terrified. Syble would do it too. Snatch her up and turn her over to her brother. He'd kill her this time because Syble would make up some story about her holding out on her. Allen enjoyed it too much to kill when provoked.

"Carrie, it's Knox. Let me in, please." She told him to go away. "I'm not leaving until I see you. Come on, your sister is gone, and I'm here to see you. You can trust me to let me in. I just want to make sure you're all right."

She unlocked the door and fell into his arms, sobbing. Christ, that was close, and now that her family had figured out where she lived, she was no longer safe in this place. And she so loved it here.

"I'm going to call the others. You can't stay here any longer." She nodded between bursts of tears. "Come on, honey, let me sit you down so that I can make a few calls. We'll get you out of here tonight. You're going to be just fine."

No, she wasn't. They were going to find her and make her pay for them missing Mom's monthly checks. It wasn't as though she was getting them either, but the nursing home was. It wouldn't matter to them where the money was going, she was the reason for it not being in their pockets, and that's all they would care about. Christ, she was going to die after finding something that she was good at. Working for the Ericksons.

Chapter 6

Georgie didn't care for being in a jail cell. She had been in and out of jail since she'd been about ten, so it wasn't this jail that she hated but them in general. This one wasn't too bad. It was clean, and there were certain things about it that made it seem homey. But she didn't want homey, she wanted out. And the sooner the better.

"When is the judge coming to town? You said it would be this week sometime." She'd been asking every day about this supposed judge coming to town and setting up so that the few people in the cells could get their day in court. "I shouldn't be in here anyway. I know my rights."

"He'll be here tomorrow. But I'd not count on getting to see him. He's going to be taking people in order of arrest. You're way down on that list." She asked him who she had to blow to get to the top of the list. "Christ, what a thought. Nobody is gonna want you to go…when was the last time you brushed your teeth? You're disgusting. You'll have your time when it's your time. Your brother will have his time before you do."

He walked away, shivering at the thought of her going down on him. It didn't matter if her teeth were brushed or not; it was the end result that got her what she wanted. Leaning back on the wall where her cot was, she thought about everything that she'd learned about Mandy. The woman was going to regret taking her kids from her brother. She was going to raise them, and that was final. The money would be awesome, and she wondered if she could get some of the perks that her brother had while married to Betsey. A house and all the money could come in handy right now.

Betsey hadn't been a bad person to Samuel. Samuel had been a right bastard to her, however. There were times when she could almost feel sorry for the other woman. Not that she'd help her out, no that would just bring his anger down on her, but she did feel for her when Samuel set his sights on beating the shit out of her. And them boys too. She wondered if it was true that Betsey would hide them around the neighborhood to keep Samuel from hurting them. It would be just like her to do something like that.

Nobody had kept her from being knocked around when she'd been a kid. Hell, even now, she had to learn how to hold her own when Samuel was in a mood. Her parents, long gone thankfully, didn't hold back either when they had some kind of beef with her or someone else. She was convenient for them and they had about used her all up.

Samuel, too, but as he got bigger, they tended to leave him alone. That's when they'd take their worst temper out on her. When Samuel wasn't around for them. She was bigger now, too, and men didn't bother her much anymore either. Not to mention, she carried a weapon now, and that would end any kind of argument they had with her.

"Georgie, you there?" She asked her brother where else she'd be. "I was just thinking about them boys of mine. When you get out, you're going to raise them to be just like us, right? Not taking any shit from anyone around? I don't want me any pussy boys running around."

"I'll raise them to be just like we were raised. Maybe a little worse for wear on them, but they'll turn out all right. Why you asking?" He told her, shouting over the other inmates in the little jail. "Nah, I've not turned all mushy on you. Just waiting for my turn to see the judge in the next couple of days. They said that you'd be out before me. You thinking of collecting them up too?"

"They're my kids, ain't they?" She didn't say anything else when he didn't. "I got me an idea that I'm not going to be getting out of here anytime soon. My lawyer said that they're going to toss the book at me on account of me killing Betsey. It don't matter, he told me that it was her fault, I'll be the one that has to pay for her being dead."

"But like you said, it was her fault. Can't blame you if she was stupid enough to get herself killed when you were there. That could have been anyone beating her to shit." He said that he'd been caught and he'd said some things when the police arrived. "Like what? You mean about killing the boys? That's not your fault either. They were there egging you on, you tell them. I don't want you in prison, Sammy. I'm going to need you to get out so that I can figure out this welfare shit. There is a great deal that's out there that I'm going to miss out on when it comes to getting my fair share."

"You'll be just fine. I'm going to try my damnest to get out, don't get me wrong, but something you might be prepared for is me coming back here being in trouble. I don't know how long they can keep me, but I'll only be right here if you need me. And who knows, something might happen that sets me free sometime. You never know. You know they're building a new jail. I might get lost in the shuffle of them moving me around. You just never know."

She'd heard that too. Not about him being lost in the shuffle, but that they were building a new jail. She didn't see anything wrong with the one that they were in, but then she wasn't up on what sort of rules there were in building one and the new rules in place to house inmates.

The next morning, people were being shuffled out of their cells and onto a big bus. She saw her brother for the first time since being arrested and thought that he looked terrible. He needed a haircut, not to mention he looked like he'd lost about fifty pounds, weight that he could ill afford. When he waved at her, she waved back. Boy oh boy, he looked like a hard wind could knock him over without much in the way of effort.

She was told to be ready that things were going faster than they thought. When she asked about her brother, she wasn't given any information on what happened at his hearing. She was almost afraid to know, what with him looking so poorly. But by the time five rolled around, she was told she wasn't going to be able to see the judge until the next morning. Whatever. She knew that she'd be getting out on account of her not having done anything but a bit of trespassing. Weren't no cause for her being in jail for that all this time.

When the bus brought a bunch of the inmates back, she didn't see her brother. No amount of asking or threatening would get her any answers, either. As soon as the lights were out, she started yelling down at the end of the lane to get his attention, to no avail. Damn it all to fuck and back, where was he?

The next morning wasn't getting her any closer

to getting answers either. He either got into more trouble and they sent him on to prison or something else had happened to him. There wasn't any way that she was going to let it go either. She had to know where he was, or there wasn't going to be any peace for anybody.

Finally, it was her turn, and she asked the judge straight up what had happened to her brother. He looked pissed off for a minute and she didn't care. It was her only family left, and she wasn't going to have him tossed away like they do some inmates. He asked her what business it was of hers.

"He's my brother, and I'm responsible for him. Wherever you put him, I need to know." The judge shuffled some papers around on his desk, looking for a file or something. "He was in here for supposedly killing his wife. When it was all her fault. After living with him for all those years, she should know not to rile him up more when he was pissed off." She was told to watch her language. "I won't. This here is serious business. He's missing, and I want to know what you did with him. He no more killed Betsey than I did. She harped on him, and that's what got her killed."

"I remember him. He also asked to kill off his sons who were present when she was murdered as well. Asked officers of the law to turn their backs so that he could end their lives as well." She told the judge that was a lie. "A lie? I don't think so, young lady. I have six witnesses to the fact that he said those very words to them. If not for their aunt, he might well have harmed them in some way."

"She's stolen them from me. I'm going to raise them and get the benefits that Betsey had. It's not fair that she gets them when my brother is the one that knocked Betsey up and got them." He told her to watch her mouth. "Why should I? They're gonna be my brats as soon as you get your thumbs out of your butt and turn them over to me. They're mine to raise."

The gavel came down quickly, and she jumped a little. "Now you see here. I'm running things today and not you. I'll say where those boys go. And I have. I've given temporary custody to their aunt Mandy." Georgie told him that he'd better be taking that back, that she'd hate for him to get hurt. "Are you threatening me, missy? If so, there are ways to get you into trouble too. I'll not stand to be threatened in my own courtroom."

"Well, then get your head out of your ass and do what's right. I want them boys to live with me. I didn't do shit wrong to end up here in the first place. Those people got a burr up their asses like you do and called the cops on me. Trespassing? What kind of crime is that anyway? I should be able to stand and walk where I want to. I pay my taxes, too." She didn't. Georgie hadn't had a job where she got paid above the table since she was sixteen. Working to pay taxes was for the fools that liked getting money back. She just cut out the middleman and got money back for not working at all. She was living the American dream.

"Let's just see how you like waiting on me to come around again, young lady. I'm remanding you over for the next time I come to town." He banged his little hammer again, like that was law or something. She was still complaining as they were dragging her out of the room and back onto the bus. And she still had no idea where her brother was.

"He's been sent to a bigger jail. There is no hope for him getting a trial around here on account of him killing someone around here that the town liked." She asked the cop what that was supposed to mean. "It means he's going to be going to prison with the big timers. He should have kept his mouth shut, same as you. Now you're both in deep water, and there isn't going to be a thing that either of you two can do about it. Besides that, Miss Wilson had about as full custody as I have of my own children. You people need to keep your mouths closed, and things might well go your way. Not that I see it going your way now, you've done messed up. Samuel is going to be spending the rest of his life in prison, and it looks like you're going to be right there with him."

Since she didn't know what to think about that, she did keep her mouth shut. Once she was back at the jail, she was able to get more answers from the others who had been there. They were right in saying that he'd been sent to a bigger jail, more like a prison. And not only did that happen, but he was going to be awaiting a trial for his involvement in not just killing his stupid wife but the attempted murder of his sons and sister-in-law too.

It was just unfair of them to have this sort of thing happen to her brother. He was an all right guy when he wasn't drinking—she'd tried already and wasn't able to get any beer into him or herself since being here. More than likely, that was why he'd lost so much weight. He wasn't getting his nutrition from a can or two with each meal. Heads were going to roll if they didn't get up off their asses and help them out. What did they do that was so terrible? So, Betsey was dead. It wasn't like she was an upstanding citizen either. She was on welfare, and that should have given her a bad name, too. People? She just didn't understand them at all.

When dinner was brought to her, she was told that she had a visitor. Since she didn't want to miss her food, she opted to sit in her cell and talk to the other person. She was shocked when it was Mandy. But she wasn't alone. She had some big guy with her. His name was Demitrius Erikson. Whatever the hell that meant.

"I've come to tell you that I'm getting married. Soon. And once I am, we're going to adopt the boys, both Teddy and Martin." She said that wasn't going to happen. "Oh, but it is. The judge told me that once I was stable in a relationship with Demi, we could adopt the boys so that they'd have a good and stable home."

"You mean living in one of those government homes." She said that Demi had a house that was theirs that they were all four going to live in. "So you're not going to be taking advantage of the shit that's out there for you. Are you stupid or what? It's there, you should be taking as much from the government as you can. I sure would be."

"No, we're going to be on our own. The boys are happy and healthy. They don't have to worry about their father or you anymore, and I hope they grow up to be outstanding citizens. Maybe even president someday." Georgie told her that she was just sucking up. "To who? I have everything that I need to get by in life. Especially since you and Samuel are going to be going away for a long time."

"They only got me on trespassing. I don't think they put people away for that dummy." She said they were exhuming the bodies of their parents. "Who said they could do something like that? You tell them to stop that right now. They're dead and buried. There is no reason to be digging them up after all this time."

"Your reaction makes me think that we should have dug them up sooner. I know that my sister always thought that you guys killed them off. Tell me, Georgie, did you do it all alone or did your brother help you? It would do my heart good to know that both of you were going to get life in prison." She told her that she'd better be thinking about what she was doing. "Oh, I am. I'm thinking really hard on what I'm doing. I'll do what it takes to keep you and Samuel out of our lives for the rest of yours."

"You bitch. You're going to regret ever meeting me." She said that she already did. "Good. You go on being regretful all the time."

That sounded better in her head. It seemed like she was forever having that trouble. Things coming out of her mouth before she had a chance to make sure they didn't sound stupid. When she laughed, Georgie stood up and slammed her body against the bars. She was a big girl, so slamming her body against them made them shake a little. Good, maybe she'd keep that up to get out of here.

~*~

Demi knew that Mandy was still upset with him. He was at himself, too. But she was at least talking to him, and that was more than he could have hoped for at this time. She was also talking to him about his home and how she'd move back in when things were settled. He didn't dare ask what settled meant, but he was hoping that he could get her back in the house before Samuel or his sister were free. And that was looking more and more like it wasn't going to happen anytime soon.

The judge had pulled them aside and told them what they needed to do to adopt Martin and Teddy. It wasn't a long list, most of it they'd already done. Like establishing a home for the two of them. Getting them into school or some kind of educational structure. Also, to put them in a place, not necessarily a home, but a loving and settled kind of family. His did that for them. Then he suggested that they get on their way to getting married. Mandy didn't think that was fair. Single people adopted all the time, but he said that since they were already sharing a home, it wouldn't be that far of a leap to get them to take the next step. She said that she'd have to think about it. So that was where they were now.

"I have to get with that attorney that called here and let him know that Georgie's reaction was far more than it should have been for her having nothing to do with her parents' deaths." Demi asked if she thought that they'd both been killed by them. "I have no reason to doubt his thoughts on that. If they did both kill them, or even just Georgie, then they'll put her away as well. I know that the judge is one of those three times you lose sort of people. He said that Samuel and Georgie both have spent time in prison before. I just don't understand how they think that they can get the kids and all the benefits of welfare too. Like they're entitled to it or something."

"They more than likely think that they are entitled to it. It's free to them, and others are getting it, so why shouldn't they?" She told him that was just crazy. "Are you still going to put the money you get for keeping them in the bank? I think that's a wonderful idea. They can use it when they head off to college or something."

"That was my plan. I'm not going to force them to go to college, but I'm going to be very disappointed if they don't go. They need to make something of themselves for their mom's sake. She gave up a lot for them to be free to make the decision to go or not." She had too. She gave up her life to protect them both. "That reminds me. I need to call and get her headstone set up. I've been saving for it since I've been working for your family. I have enough now."

"I would have given it to you." She told him that she had it now, but was grateful for him saying that. "If you need anything else, just let me know. I have enough funds to keep you and the boys in whatever you need."

"They're not going to be spoiled. Just putting

that out there. They're going to work for what they want, and I'm not going to be giving them anything and everything that they want. I don't want them to have it all so that they're spoiled rotten kids like some rich families are."

"I agree with you on that. I don't think that any of us will spoil our kids. We've had to do without. I don't mean that we won't give them things that they need, especially for school, but I don't want them to be rotten any more than you do. They'll get what they need and, like you said, work for the rest." She nodded, and he could see her mind working on that, too. What sort of things they'd give them to make their lives better, but not too much.

Demi didn't have anything. Not even a new car. He'd gotten himself a second-hand car when he'd needed it, and he'd not gotten himself any new clothing in years. He wore what he had until it wasn't even fit for a rag. It was just the way they were. Locke even bought second-hand, too, and he had all kinds of money. But he thought of things now.

They needed a more reliable car to get the boys back and forth to school. Also, the house was about half-filled out, and he wanted them to have their own things. Taking the bunk beds from the little house had been on his list of things to do, just so they'd have more room in their own rooms. Also bikes. The two that they had were rusty and worn, and he was afraid they'd get hurt from them. There were a great many things that he wanted to get for them that were a necessity.

He started a list of things that he wanted to take care of, and he noticed that Mandy had one as well. They needed new backpacks. The ones that they'd been given were in bad shape, and he thought that one of them had been his when he'd been taking classes at the university. They needed one better than he'd had.

"I have things that I can use for the house at the little one if you'd not mind bringing them over." He asked her what they might be. "Well, one thing that I need is the coffee maker. It arrived just before I left here, and I've not set it up. I do need a cup of coffee once in a while, and it's a really nice one. Also, there is the couch in the living room. It'll be too small by itself in your living room, but it's at least something we can sit on. There are lamps, too."

After they'd gone over their lists, he was impressed at how much she wanted to bring to the big house. There were things that they were going to have to buy, extra towels and linens and such, but they had plenty of time to get some of the things that the boys needed too, like computers. They would need them to do their homework on. A great many of the classes they were going to take were online and could be done at their own pace. He loved that idea, too.

Demi also made sure that she had some credit cards with her name on them. He only had the three major ones and hadn't felt like getting anything more after Alex had gone through their credit when she'd first come to the family and gotten them narrowed down on what they were spending money on each month. He'd been spending money on two cable accounts in the same home. And one of the others had been paying to have his suits pressed monthly when he didn't even wear a suit to the tune of five grand per month. They'd been had, and thankfully, she'd been able to get things taken care of for them in less time than he would have thought. He knew that he'd put it off until he forgot about it again.

There had also been a limo service that they were being charged for, which none of them used. They would have driven or walked to most of the things and places that they needed to go. He would be forever grateful to her for looking outside the box for them.

"Mr. Demi? Can we just call you Demi?" He told Teddy that he'd like that too. "I know you're not our dad on account of you being nice and all but someday we might want to do that too. You're way nicer than he ever was to us. Aunt Mandy said it would be up to you what we called you. Is that all right?"

"It is. Calling me Mr. Demi makes me feel kind

of old." Martin pointed out that he was old, and he tickled him until he screamed. "What do you call my brothers? Mr. Locke? I think it's safe to assume that they're going to be your uncles soon, so you can call them that. I know you call Alex your aunt."

"Yeah, she said that calling her Miss Alex made her feel like she needs to be having a lot of cats. I love cats, so I don't understand that." He told him that he should ask her sometimes. "I will, but she uses big words and I don't understand her any more than I did before. Aunt Shipley kind of scares us. I don't think that she'd hurt us, but she always has a gun, and that's sort of scary to the two of us." Martin nodded like his head was on a bobble. "Aunt Mandy is the best to us. She sits us down and talks to us about everything. I'm glad. She even explains things so that we understand them too. All kinds of stuff. I asked her for a dog and she sat us down and told us that a dog is a lot of responsibility and that if we wanted one, we was going to have to work for it. That's what we're doing. Showing her how we can be responsible human beings before we can be responsible for another being. I love that she called us human beings. Because you know why? Cause that's what we are. Isn't that funny?"

"That is funny. And I agree with her about being responsible for something else. That's a good plan to have." Martin said they already had a name picked out for it. Snoopy. "That is a great name. I like it." Mandy had made two kids who hadn't had a thing in their lives want something to take care of. And he had no doubt that they'd do a good job of it, too, simply because of how they were being raised.

Something that he'd been asking himself since she'd moved back into his house, and he'd realized that he loved her, was why he ever thought that he didn't. Every day since then, he'd been finding new ways that he loved her, new things that would have him gushing about how wonderful she was. Christ, he loved her with every breath he took.

She made it easy, too, to love her. She was kind, compassionate, and loving. She took care too that those around her had what they needed from her and then some. She was also happy. He loved hearing her singing through the house. While she was outside with the boys or simply hanging out with him. She gave joy wherever she was, and he loved every bit of her.

Tonight they were having make-your-own pizza. And he was looking forward to that more than he was any six-course meal that he could have whipped up. It was the simple things in life that were giving him such joy now, and he didn't even care who called him a sap.

Chapter 7

The house was settling into a good routine. He didn't like it, but that seemed to be making the rest of the residents of the house happy, so he went along with it. He wanted things to shake up, to be fun. But with two kids in the house and a woman who seemed to be a little upset with him most of the time, he was going with it. Demi hated routine.

For as much as he loved things organized, he didn't care for getting up at seven in the morning, taking a shower, eating, and going out the door. He supposed that he was bored. That's what it was, he told himself, he was bored. And he was going to get himself in trouble if he didn't stick with being bored all the time.

While he didn't want anyone mad at him, he did need something more. Maybe a little play in the morning before getting a shower. Not sex, though that would be fantastic, but something to happen that would make everyone smile throughout the day when they thought about it. Something...just something. He was so going to be in trouble. Especially if he kept thinking the way that he was.

Demi didn't want chaos. He just wanted something to shake things up. To giggle a little. He kept telling himself that he could do this. It could be boring, but every day, he thought of something else to do, to shake things up a bit. One of these mornings, he was going to bust loose and do it. However he was afraid that everyone would be pissed off at him for messing up their routine. Deciding to talk to his brothers, he left the house before the kids were finished with breakfast and went in search of any one of them to talk to.

"Don't do it." Locke just happened to be the one that he found first, and after telling him his dilemma, his brother was shaking his head even before he finished speaking. "You'll upset everyone, and I'm sure that's not what you want. Have you gone completely mad? Seriously, Demi, don't do it. Not only will you regret it, but you'll regret it for a long time. Wives have long memories and they'll remember that shit long after the kids are grown and out of the house. They'll be calling you the bad guy."

"For wanting a little fun? When did you get to be an old man? It's not like I'm going to go out and murder someone. I'm just going to interject a little fun in the morning. I think you're looking at this all wrong. Don't you ever mess up Alex's routine in the morning?" He nodded and said that she'd messed it up, not him. "So, if you want a little sex in the morning, you have to wait for her to start it? That doesn't sound like you at all."

"All I can tell you is not to do it." He went to find another brother. But on his way to find someone else, his cell phone rang. It was Mandy.

"Why did you leave so early?" He decided to come clean. He told her everything that he'd been thinking. "Oh, thank goodness. I thought you were mad at us. No, I don't mind a little bit of a routine buster. But the boys need calm before they go to school."

"Is that written down someplace? I mean, I remember us being at home and...never mind, that's not a good example. But when I was going to college while living with Martha, some mornings I'd barely get out the door on time because...that's not a good example either. Damn it, I want them to have fun. Why can't they have fun before going to school? A food fight would be — again, not good. I don't know what I want. I just think they'd benefit from a little laughter before tackling school. I'm coming — wait. Why did you think I was mad at you?"

"You left without telling me goodbye. You usually...you know you're just as much in a routine as we are. You have your alarm set for a certain time that gets you up and going too." He told her that tomorrow he was going to take them to breakfast. "I don't know about that. It'll be—"

"It'll be a blast. We'll get up earlier than usual, take them to breakfast, and have a few laughs. That will make me feel better." She asked him if he knew what they did in the morning. "We go over homework. Yes, I'm aware of the way we do things. And I think one morning we can skip going over homework for the tenth time and just enjoy each other. If you want, we can tell them tonight what we're doing and they won't be so surprised about the change. But I'm telling you right now, Mandy, I need something to shake up our lives. Before I go insane."

"All right. But if they're upset, I'm going to blame you." He told her that he was willing to take that blame if it got them to get together as a family. "It does sound like it'll be fun. I mean, it's been a while since we've done anything like a family does."

He thought that having her on board was half the battle in this. And if he messed up too much, then he wouldn't ask them again. Well, he might, but not as much as he did this time. He turned the car around and headed home. There were plans to make, and he was going to get started on them right away.

"Where did you go?" Demi told Teddy that he had to talk to his brother. "I have to talk to mine sometimes, too, but I don't run off without saying goodbye to everyone. I thought I'd done something to make you mad at me."

"Why would you think that? I mean, I'm usually out the door before you're even awake when I have to go to the restaurant. You didn't think I was mad then, did you?" Teddy told him he'd not seen him, so it didn't count. "How about tomorrow we all go out for breakfast instead of being here and eating. That'll be fun, don't you think?"

"How will I be able to go over my homework? I have to make sure that it's all right." He asked him if he'd gotten a bad grade so far. "No. Because we go over it a lot. I can even answer questions when the teacher asks. I love doing that. It makes me feel like I'm smart."

"You are smart." He pointed out that it was because he went over his homework a lot. "Teddy, work with me here. I need to do this so I can feel good about having a family."

"We're still your family, Demi. It's just that the morning is for homework and stuff. I don't want the teacher to think I'm slacking again. When Dad was around, I was forever slacking. On account of I couldn't get my homework done and stuff. I love being able to tell the teacher we went over our homework—"

"I give up." Teddy asked him if he was upset. "No. Just resigned to the fact that you're an old fuddy duddy and I'm going to be doing things the same way until you're out of college." He tousled the boy's hair.

"I should have known it wouldn't work. There is just too much going on in the morning for it to happen."

"But you make my whole day by being here and helping me. I think about it all the time that you and my aunt have made it so that Martin and I have a safe place to live and sleep. We didn't get much sleep when my dad was around. Now, not only do we sleep, but we get to have showers and snacks. You have no idea how happy it makes me when I can get up and go to the fridge and there is food there for us to eat. That the milk isn't spoiled, or I have to tear off mold from bread to have a sandwich." He started to tell him how sorry he was, but Teddy was on a roll now. "Something else that makes me feel good is that I have clothing that's all mine. It fits and it's clean. One time when the washer broke down, Momma couldn't do laundry for a whole month until her check came in. The kids made fun of us all the time for being the stinky boys. I like the way things are because they were never like this at home. I never knew if I was going to get lunch or not. I never knew if Momma was going to feel like getting up with us. She didn't help with our homework; she was too busy trying to get dad to stop beating on us."

Demi felt like a heel. Here he wanted something to shake his day up, and the kids just wanted things to be normal. Daily things that they knew were there so that they could have a good day. Going over homework seemed so boring to him, but it was perfect for the kids. He should have known that and should have taken into consideration how they had lived before, when he was only thinking of himself.

There was no reason that he couldn't make them laugh in the mornings or be silly about homework. He could do those things for them. He would do those things for them just so he could think about them throughout his own day and smile. Giving the kids stability was more important than having a day start off differently than the one before. They needed him to be there for them and he would from now on. They were depending on him, and he was going to make sure that he was there for them.

He got to take the kids to school most mornings, so he was going to make that his time with them. Find something along the path that they took so that they could examine it. A pine cone or something like that to marvel at. He could have his routine messed up a little if he wanted, but not at the expense of the kids having their routine just the way they wanted it.

The rest of his morning and into the afternoon, he worked on his next project. The restaurant was running nicely and didn't need him there all the time. Now that it had been turned over to capable hands, he was ready to start something new. Something that would benefit his sons. Because at the end of the day, they were his sons as much as Mandy was going to be his wife.

That got him thinking about a ring for her. He had three that had been left to him from Martha. The one he was thinking about would be beautiful on her hand. It had special meaning to him as well. Martha had worn it to his college graduation and told him then that someday it would be his to use with his own wife.

The yellow diamond had gone well with the dress that she'd worn that day. Her happiness had been infectious, and he still remembered the check that she'd given him when he'd been going off to have some fun with his other classmates.

"You use this money for fun, young man. And I do mean it." He told her that every day was fun to him, and she'd laughed. "Someday you'll meet a young woman and you'll want to get her something special. Use this money for that. Don't ever cut corners with buying someone you love something lovely, Demitrius. It will be a remembrance for the two of you for the rest of your lives."

He decided that he needed to go to a jeweler and figure out something special for Mandy. As he was thinking about what he wanted in the way of a ring, the first one he thought of kept coming back to him. It would be perfect.

The yellow diamond was surrounded by

smaller white diamonds in a beautiful setting that he loved. The band was wide and made of platinum. It had been cleaned when he'd gotten it and now only needed to be sized. Mandy had such tiny fingers he knew that he'd have to be careful in getting the size right. Then he realized that he could just take her to get it sized, and he'd not have to worry about getting it right. Christ, there were times when he outthought himself on things.

He was deep in thought about the ring when Knox found him. The two of them had been meeting up for lunch on Thursdays for the past ten years or so. He got together with his other brothers, too, but for some reason, meeting up with Knox was the highlight of his week. Today was no different.

"I need a new project, and I'm betting you have an idea what I should be working on." He asked him if he'd been to the school board meeting last night. "No. I didn't even know there was one. I need to pay more attention to what's going on. The boys go there."

"They're having trouble keeping people employed to do the morning breakfast program. It's the first hot meal some of these kids get before lunch comes around, and that one isn't always hot. They need five cooks willing to come in and do it. Do you know anyone who might have experience in cooking for a lot of kids?" Demi asked him what it meant in the way of a cook. "Mostly just what you think. Eggs mostly. Sometimes they have cereal when there isn't enough money for eggs and sausage. But for the most part, you'd be cooking for about two hundred kids in the morning, then go home. There isn't even any clean up as the lunch ladies do that, so they don't have to come in earlier for that shift."

"I take it that it doesn't pay well." He told him what was the going rate was, and Demi whistled. "That's a lot of money. Why don't they just let me do the cooking and then use the money for — why are you shaking your head?"

"You would need to be paid. It's a paid position, so not getting paid would cause all kinds of issues. You can donate the money back in some other way, but you would get paid." Demi thought that was silly and told his brother that. "Silly or not, it's the rules that they have to abide by. Anyway, you would go in and cook, feed the kids, then leave. The hot breakfast consists of eggs, of course, sausage or ham, toast, and some kind of packaged jelly. There is milk and juice when they can afford that, too. It's pretty standard. And you get to hang out with the kids every day. I know you're kind of sappy like that."

"I like to hang out with my kids every day. Two hundred of them would make me crazy." Knox told him that he thought he'd love it. "I didn't say

I wouldn't, but that's a lot of kids to take under my wing. When can I start?"

"Since you've already had a background check, you can start tomorrow. I wouldn't think you'd need all that much help, being that you know how to cook for a lot of people. And you might well not have all that much help. I'll come and work with you. I think it would be fun, and I'll see if I can get two more people on board to help us out. I would think that cracking the eggs would be the most help you'd need, right?" He said that making the toast would be helpful as well. "I forgot about that. Hopefully, there is more than a couple of two-slice toasters."

"If not, then we'll bake them. I can do this if you help, but we will need a couple more people. Maybe a couple of the women would come in and help us out. I know that they all have jobs, but if we ask nicely, maybe they'll be willing to carve out some time to help out." Knox pulled out his cell phone and called someone. "Also, I don't know anything about the kitchen. I'll need to go over there soon to get the lay of it. I don't want to mess up anything by having to look for things that I might need."

By the time he was off the phone, all three of the wives were going to help him. They couldn't do it daily, but one of them would show up to help out. Then they were headed to the school so that he could figure out where things were and get to know the women that he'd kind of be working with. Demi was as excited about this as he'd been anything in a while. He also knew that once he got it started, he'd not let it go like he did most of his other projects. This way, he'd be able to see his boys, too, even though they didn't eat at the school, they'd be there.

The kitchen wasn't as organized as he had hoped it would be, but that was fine. He was learning a valuable lesson in not changing things around because they didn't suit him. Once breakfast was served and everything put away, he was free for the rest of the day, and that excited him a great deal. Yes, he thought this was going to be a fun thing for him to do, and he was helping the schools out as well.

~*~

"How many gallons of milk does your family drink in a month's time? I mean, five gallons seems like a lot to me." Mrs. Harris told her that she could only drink one a week, but wanted the rest sent to her weekly. "I'm afraid that if you order five gallons, they're going to be delivered all at the same time."

"No, that won't work for me. You'll have to tell them to bring them to me weekly." She tried explaining to her again how it will take weekly orders when you order them, but it will all be delivered at once when you tell them what you want. "You just tell them that they can't do it that way. I only want one gallon per week."

They'd been going over this every day for two weeks now, on how she wanted things delivered, over her putting in an order for what she wanted. It was becoming annoying as hell for her, too. Usually very patience with people Mrs. Harris was an entitled bitch and had to mess up the way she was teaching every time.

"Look, Helen, she's told you this so many times that everyone in the room gets it but you. I honestly think that you get it, you just like being trouble. This might have worked in high school or even at your own home, but this is class, and you're taking up time from the rest of us. Just order it like you're supposed to and shut the hell up. You're giving me a headache." June Paddle had her laughing behind her hand again. The woman had no filter at all. "Damned woman. I bet the plants could order your groceries by now, and they ain't even real."

"I don't like this ordering from a computer at all. I don't know why I'm being made to do this." Mandy told Helen that no one was forcing her to order her groceries, but she had signed up for the class. "I thought it would be fun to get out of the house for an hour or two, but all you do is keep telling me what I can't do instead of what I want to do. I don't care for being told no, you know. Why can't you just let me — "

"Don't you dare say you need five gallons of milk a month to me again, you old bat. There ain't nobody at your house but you and that old woman that you have to clean up after you. Hell, I'm betting that she finds herself a nice dark corner to get away from your harping all the time and takes a nap. That's what I'd do if I had to hang around you for more than ten seconds. You're nothing but a harpy, Helen, and everyone here knows it."

"I do, too, need to have five gallons of milk. I need it to feed the cats, now don't I? You need to mind your own business, June. There ain't nobody talking to you." June asked her how many cats she had. "I have about a dozen of them now on the inside, and that many more that just shows up. I don't give them all milk, but those that want it, it's there for them."

"Two dozen cats. Good heavens Helen no wonder you smell like cat piss all the time. What are they doing? Running the house for you? Nobody needs that many cats. Good Christ, love a duck, that sure does explain a lot." Helen asked her what she meant by that. "Mr. Harris run off, didn't he? More than likely because you had all them cats that you're taking care of."

Now there were insults being hurled around the room like cake at a party. Mandy sat down at her little desk, knowing that things were out of control for her to get anything done. All the women, all five of them, were yelling at each other, insults were being fired off like it was their job. When one of the women sat down beside her, she smiled at Mrs. Rogan.

"They sure do go on, don't they, honey?" She just smiled and told her she tries to stay out of it. "Don't blame you one bit. Not a bit. I do have me a question. It ain't about milk but when they don't have something. I don't want them to send me something of equal value. The other week they sent me a grater and I have plenty enough of those. I just want what I order and if they don't have it, take it off my bill. Can I do that?"

"Yes, but they'll have to give you a store credit rather than your money back. Is that all right?" She told her it was better than having a dozen or so cheese graters lying around. "Yes, I can see where that would be a problem. I'll show you how to set it up for yourself. Do they run out of things that often?"

She answered her that they didn't do it often, but once was enough. After showing her how to change the settings on the order page, she went back to her seat. After a few minutes, another woman came up to get her questions answered. This went on for the rest of the class. She was answering questions on the side while the other woman fought about cats and milk. It was almost too much for even her to deal with.

When the timer went off twice, alerting them that the class had ended, the two women who had the most to say left, still fighting over the milk issue. She didn't want either one of them back and was glad that the classes they were in, a four-week class, were finished for them. They would either sink or swim as far as she was concerned. Having something for her headache in her drawers at the office, she stopped by there to get some. That was when she ran into Shipley. She told her how the class was today when she asked.

"I heard them arguing as they were leaving. Is that normal?" She told her that for those two women, it was very normal. "I would have pulled out my gun and ended the argument right then. I don't like bickering for the sake of bickering. So are you ready for the next set of women? These are all six domestics that need to learn how to do it for the household."

"I am. But something was brought up today. It's about missing items." She told her that two of the women today didn't want the store to give them something of equal value, and how they didn't need whatever they were giving. "I can see where that might be an issue. I'd say make it up in food, it would be eaten at my house, but then I have kids in the house, and most of the women in the classes do not."

"Yeah, I understand that too." After talking a bit more on that subject, Shipley brought up the breakfast at the school and how they were going to go and help out Demi tomorrow. "You can come too. It'll be fun to see the kids having a nice, hot meal, and Demi seemed very excited when I talked to him later. It's a program that, as a charity-based doner, we can really get behind. He's thinking that he could make a good breakfast without a lot of trouble."

"He's used to cooking for a lot of people. I believe that the people in there before weren't at all used to cooking for more than their family. I think that was the bottleneck they were running into." Shipley agreed with her on that. "I'm to understand that the state pays for the food to be given out. Is that right? Maybe with his background, he could get them better deals on the food that is coming in."

"I never thought of that." Shipley smiled at her. "I love it when I get to talk to you. You always make me see things that I don't normally get to see. Thanks for that."

"My pleasure. So I'll be there at the school in the morning. Maybe the boys will want to eat there, too, so they can see Demi. They do love that man." Shipley told her that they all loved him. "So do I."

After getting ready for the classes starting tomorrow, she was surprised to find Carrie in the office. She'd heard that she'd been moved again, the poor woman had some family much like hers. But the difference was that hers was in jail right now, where Carries were running around causing trouble for everyone.

"I've been so careful about looking around for them. That's exhausting too." She asked her where she was staying now. "In a hotel. It's not fun, but at least I'm safe. I'm fearful that if they find me now, they'll kill me because Mom's checks are going straight to the nursing home. And she is doing so well there, I'd hate for her to have to give that up."

"I don't blame you. My grandmother was in a nursing home right up until she died. She loved being able to be social when she wanted, and she could close her door when she didn't. I think she lived longer too, simply because she had interaction with others around her same age." Carrie told her that her mom was slipping away from her more and more, and that was sad, but she was glad that she was someplace safe. "Safe is about all you can hope for with families like ours, don't you think?"

They talked about that for another hour until Carrie had to get back to her desk. She'd not realized that a car came to take her back and forth to work. It was another annoyance she told her, but again, she wasn't out there where her brother Allen could find her. She'd heard about him, he was a monster.

Mandy cleaned off her desk of post-it notes and

other notes that she'd made throughout her day. She felt a sense of accomplishment when she only had one or two notes left to finish at the end of the day. Today, even with everything that was going on, she'd been able to knock all of them off her desk in record time. Tomorrow would be a bit harder as she was going to be at the school first thing in the morning with the boys and Demi.

She so loved that man and was disappointed that he seemed to be avoiding her when it came to bedtime. She wanted to jump his bones every evening, but he came to bed a great deal later than she did, and it was impossible to do anything with the boys hanging on his every word. They loved him as well, but—

"I have a question." She told Alex she was all ears. "Have you and Demi done the nasty yet?"

The question and what she'd been thinking threw her off for a few seconds. Long enough for her to be sputtering around with a non-answer. But Alex seemed to have understood and nodded. Long enough, too, that she had a plan to remedy her lack of sex.

"I thought so. The way the two of you look at each other is hot and all, but it's very difficult to get together when there are others around, like the boys. I want you guys to think of a honeymoon after you're married. As a family, we own this little island paradise that the two of you could go to and unwind. We did it and it was the best week I've ever spent in my life. You'll have to go there soon."

"I don't want to pawn off the boys to anyone." She said it would be their pleasure to watch over them. "How about we go after this thing with Georgie is taken care of. She's sort of putting a damper on everything we think to do. I can't wait for her to be sent to prison like my brother-in-law has been."

"Great idea. I love that even better. All right, but it will have to be just as soon as it's done with her. If there were ever two people who needed less stress in their lives, it would be the two of you."

Plans were made and things were set up. Shipley had purchased the island home a couple of months back, and she and Locke had been making the trip to it weekly to get things set up for family. She couldn't wait to tell Demi about it and get there. They really did need less stress in their lives right now.

Chapter 8

Demi had been working outdoors for the past two days. His body was aching and sore from all the extra activity, but he wasn't sleeping any better. He wanted Mandy, but did promise her that he'd never push her into anything she wasn't ready for. His heart said he was doing the right thing; however, his mind and body didn't agree with him. Stepping into the cold shower again, all he could think about was that Mandy was only a few doors down the hall from where he was right now.

"Demi?" Shouting that he was in the shower, he prayed that no one would come into the bathroom with him. "Are you all right? I was worried because this is the third time today that you've taken a shower."

"I've been working in the yard. I'll be out in a minute." He looked down at his cock and knew that if he waited an hour it wouldn't be any different. "I'll meet you downstairs in a little bit."

"Are you all right?" She was not just in the bathroom with him, but she was standing close to the door to the shower, too. "Demi, please tell me what's wrong. I want to help."

"I'm sure you do, babe, but I'm in a bad way here." She tossed back the curtain and exposed him. "I'm sorry. So very sorry. However, I did ask you to leave me alone."

She didn't say anything for several seconds, and he blindly reached over and turned the shower off. If she didn't speak soon, he was going to be fumbling all over himself trying to tell her how —

"I didn't think that you wanted me." He laughed. It was that, or he was going to sob. "I've been trying to tell you I'm ready for you for the last week, and you would rush out the door and — I guess I'm not very good at being sexy."

"Men are very basic, honey. You should have just come out and told me that you wanted me. I've been killing myself so that I could sleep at night without going down the hall and ravaging you." She grinned at him. "This isn't funny at all. I'm hurting and taking cold showers at least twice a day to be able to function. All the blood in my body is in my cock most of the day."

"Can I help you with that?" He whimpered. There was no hope for him if she touched him right now. He was going to come all over the shower and her. "I'm not as experienced as you are with sex, but I'm betting that I could do something that would make you feel better."

"If you're teasing me right now, Mandy, I'm going to cry. I'm seriously hurting right now. One word from you and I'm not going to be responsible for what happens to you."

"Yes." It was the way she said it rather than the word. It came out like a hissing sound that seemed to curl around his buttocks then straight to his cock. When she reached out and wrapped her hand around him, he fell against the wall of the shower and let her do her worst to him. He was done trying to keep her from knowing just how needy he was. "I want to suck your cock. Would that be all right?"

He didn't remember answering. Nor did he see her move. One second she was standing in the bathroom with him, the next she was naked and in the shower stall with him. Again, he reached for the valve and turned it to what he hoped was a warmer temperature.

Leaning against the shower wall he watched Mandy as she played with his cock. Licking him up one side, then down the other, following the thick vein as it pulsated. When her tongue swirled around his crown, it was all he could do to stay upright. Her hands on his thighs were warm against his skin, and when she cupped her hands on his balls, he cried out, feeling like he was close to coming. But he didn't, holding off for the pleasure that she was giving him. Even as she fondled his balls, rolling them in her hand there was a little pain but it was so worth it to have her mouth on his cock.

Every time he thought that he was going to come, she'd sense it somehow and would change up what she'd been doing. Each time he didn't get to come, he felt a little pang of pain in his chest, like all his love was stored up there and just waiting for her to allow him to finish. Holding back, trying to make it last, was the last thing on his mind. Demi wanted to come hard enough to blast his cum all over her. Then she swallowed him past the tightness of her throat, and he cried out again.

Coming had never felt so good. Fucking her throat, harder than he should have he knew, had him emptying in her three times before she pulled away. Looking up at him, her lovely mouth bruised slightly from what they'd done, he pulled her up from the floor. Pressing her to his body he slammed his cock deep inside of her pussy even as he pressed her against the damp wall.

With her legs wrapped around him, he fucked her hard. Her fingers tangled in his hair, holding him to her mouth as he kissed her savagely. Tasting blood, he nearly backed off, but she pulled him tighter still. Lifting her up by her ass, he took her breast into his mouth and suckled hard on the pert nipple she offered him.

Demi thought that he could go this way for days, loving her, making love to her body. But her need was pounding at him so he slid his finger down her ass crack until he came to her little rose bud. Pressing against it slightly had her screaming out his name, even as he kissed her mouth to try and silence her. Nearly bucking him off, he held tightly to her until she came three more times. His own body had been used up, and now he was taking her so that he could empty deep inside of her one more time.

Neither one of them moved as he stood in the shower holding her. Her body was still coming, small tremors that had his cock staying semi hard. Lifting her up when she told him she needed to stand up, he slid from her body and picked her up in his arms. Taking her to bed, he was surprised that she'd made it when she'd come up here. Laying her on the bed, he nearly didn't make it to his own side before his body just fell forward. He was as spent as he'd ever been.

Waking up for what seemed to be only seconds, he looked at the clock and couldn't believe it was morning, and he'd slept through the afternoon and night. Reaching out to find Mandy, he realized that she'd gotten up long enough for her side of the bed to be cold. Getting into the shower again, his body aching. Again. Demi scrubbed his body from head to his feet before feeling like he'd been chopping wood for the past couple of days, and his body was telling him he'd been a fool.

Getting dressed, no easy feat with the way he was feeling, he made his way downstairs only to remember that the boys would be gone from the house already, as they'd been planning to spend the day with Shipley to learn about a gun. She was the perfect person to teach them gun safety, so he wasn't worried about them. He found Mandy in the kitchen going over a list that she'd been keeping since moving back in.

"Good morning." He kissed her, careful of the little bruise on her lip. "I was just thinking that since it's Saturday, we should get some of this list tucked away while the boys are with Shipley. She said she'd feed them lunch and keep them until four if we had things to do. Do we have things to do?"

Grinning at her, he kissed her again. "I can think of all kinds of things we can do, but I think you broke me. I know I'll never take a shower again without thinking of you." She cleared her throat, and that was when he saw their cook. Her face was pink with embarrassment, and he couldn't for the life of him summon up an apology for her. "I'd love to take you to the store to get this stuff. We've put it off long enough, I think."

"Good. I was hoping you'd say that. Let me tell Shipley where we'll be in the event something happens and we can be off." While she was on the phone, he did apologize to Grace. When she simply waved him off, he smiled at her. It was fun having someone around who could be there for a good joke or whatever. "Okay, that's taken care of. We need to get going so we can get there and back before it's too late."

Since he'd slept so late, they decided to get lunch on the way. He'd been cooking for the school for the past week and had been enjoying it a good deal more than he thought that he would. However, getting up at four in the morning was exhausting. Getting there early enough to turn the ovens on was the only reason he didn't sleep until six-thirty and feed the kids by seven-thirty.

The first day of doing it was hit-and-miss. None of the kids had been told they'd be getting breakfast, so they had actually trashed a lot of the food they cooked. However, on the second morning, there were seventy students lined up to get a hot breakfast, and twice that many more on the third day. After that, even the teachers were in line to get something to eat, and there were very few leftovers anymore. He was given permission to serve pancakes if he wanted, but he'd have to use the large grill. While he knew how to use it, he wanted someone to come in and give him a once over so he'd not mess things up for the lunch ladies that came in around nine. He'd not realized that the first lunch was served at ten-thirty.

Shopping with Mandy was fun. The things on their list, however, were boring to shop for. Napkins for the dining room. Glasses for the kitchen. He got to help pick out the things they were getting, but for the life of him, he really couldn't understand why it mattered if the napkins matched the placemats. He would have gotten all white ones and been done with it, but Mandy did have a point. White would show stains more.

There were other things on the list that he was glad to have gotten. A television for the living room was needed. They'd been watching TV when they did on a twenty-inch television that barely worked. When he said he wanted the largest one they had, the man looked skeptical, but he did show him the seventy-five-inch one that just happened to be on sale too.

Lamps for the room were a necessity as there was no overhead lighting in the room. The two of them decided that they did need fans in the living room to keep the room fresh, but they were going to have them installed. He could do it, but didn't want to fall and hurt himself. Then something occurred to him. He had the ring with him.

"I have something for you." He got down on

one knee and looked up at her. "If you don't like it for whatever reason, we can exchange it today. Will you marry me and make me happier than my sappy brothers are with their wives?"

"I didn't think that you'd—oh, Demi, it's beautiful. Did Martha leave this to you?" He told her that she had, but if she didn't like it, they were in town today and could get her something different. "No, this is perfect. I feel like she's been watching over me since I fell in love with you. Oh, Demi, it couldn't be more perfect. Yes, I'll marry you."

He'd not realized that they'd drawn a crowd, but the well wishes were wonderful from the strangers. Even when he kissed his soon-to-be wife, they applauded them both and wished them years of marital bliss.

Demi caught her looking at the ring off and on all the rest of the day. When they were finishing up, they decided to have an early dinner. Shipley had called and said they were having brats on the grill, and the boys wanted to stay again. They both thought it was a wonderful idea and went to have a nice dinner in an expensive restaurant. The rest of the evening was spent with them having the grandest time ever.

By the time they were home, the two of them were so exhausted that they weren't sure they could make it up the stairs. And they still had the truck to unload. Not to mention, put it all away.

"I'm all for leaving it in the truck and getting it tomorrow. If you pull it into the garage, things should be all right, don't you think?" Demi agreed with Mandy, telling her that they'd get it unloaded and put away first thing. "Good. Until tomorrow then. Once we get it in the house, it'll be easy to get it put away. And the things that need to be washed will have to wait until next weekend. I have a busy week, and I know you do as well."

"I knew there was a good reason that I wanted to marry you. You're brilliant." She told him he was goofy. "I'll own that, my dear. And I love you."

"I love you as well, you big lug." They were both giggling as they finally made it up the stairs. She decided that he would sleep in the big bed with her, and he couldn't have been happier. It was turning into the best day of his life.

~*~

Georgie was waiting for her turn to see the judge. She'd been last to get off the bus and was now last in line to see the stupid judge. There were things that she needed answers to and he'd better have them for her or she was going to be pissed off. Again.

The problem was that with being last, he was getting shorter and shorter with people who were ahead of her. She didn't want him pissed off when he got to her and decided that she was going to have to do something or she'd be shit out of luck getting out of the jail not to mention finding out where her brother had been taken. There was no reason why the two of them had to be separated. They were all each other had.

"I wanna go next." The officer told her that she had to wait her turn like everyone else was. "No, he'll be too pissy when he gets to me, and I have some important stuff I need answers for. I'm not going to be waiting on that again."

Standing up, she was told to sit down. Ignoring the officer for the judge, she finally got his attention. Telling him why she didn't want to wait got his attention, but not the right kind.

"Well then, you just tell me what it is you want and the rest of the people will just have to wait like normal people do." She told him she was a normal person, and he slammed his little hammer down and charged her fifty dollars for back talk. "Do it again, and we'll just see how well you like it at the beginning of the line. What do you want that can't wait another twenty minutes?"

"Where's my brother? He was in the same jail as me, and now he's gone." The judge asked her what his name was. While he was shuffling through the paperwork on his desk thingy, she remembered her next question. "When will I start seeing benefits for raising his kids, too. They're mine now, and I want a piece of the pie their mother was getting before she died."

"Samuel Jameson has been taken to a bigger jail than this one. He's up on murder charges, and they'll handle him better there." She said that he'd not been given a trial. "So? He'll get one when the date comes up. I believe it's sometime next year. July, if I remember correctly."

"That's not right. He's gotta be there for all that time? You have to change your mind about that date. He'll hate being in prison again." The judge told her that was the point. No one should like to be in prison. "Then you'll change the date for me? I need him around. I've never raised up kids before."

"Are you Georgetta Jameson?" She told him that she was just called Georgie. "Well, not today. We're usually a bit more formal when it comes to having people jailed. I have paperwork here for you, too. The bodies of yours and Samuel's parents have been exhumed, and you and your brother's DNA were all over their bodies. And who buries the weapons they were killed with in their casket? Those were found as well."

"That's not fair. I told them not to go digging them up. I know you have to have permission on digging up family members, and I didn't give it. I'm sure that Samuel didn't do it either. You tell them that it doesn't count, whatever you found, as I'm not going back to jail either. It's not fair."

"Fair or not, you're going to be remanded over to a larger prison to await your trial time as well. I have it on here somewhere that tells me when the two of you will stand trial for their murders. Here it is. December of next year." Georgie told him *fuck no*. when the man stood up and pointed his hammer at her, she knew for sure that she'd been better off waiting her turn. Right now he was about as pissed off as she'd ever seen somebody and that included her brother Samuel "Five thousand dollar fine and you'll be remanded over to the women's prison now. Telling me no and using profanity, too. I should throw the book at you now, but I'm a better man than you are a woman. I'm about to have my retirement date moved so that I can be there when you're up for trial."

She was taken away in her cuffs and shackles. Before she left the room, however, she flipped the judge off and laughed when he threw his hammer at her. It was the little things that got her through the day, and she was going to get them where she could. As soon as she was on the bus, locked down so that she couldn't move, nobody got on the bus with her after the cops left her.

"Damned idiots. What am I supposed to do here

with no phone to play on?" She watched them to see what they were going to do now. "If I had me a knife, I'd kill you both without another thought."

Another cruiser pulled up while she was waiting for them to take her back to the jail. She was beginning to like the little small town place and the good food that they served her three times a day. Also, the big comforter was nice late at night when she woke up a bit too chilly in the room.

When the other cop got out of his car, he had a bag of something, and he looked like he was in some kind of police vest. Figures, she thought, now they think I'm dangerous. When the bag was tossed to one of the officers who had been on the bus with her, they all turned and looked at her. Whatever was going on, it was somehow related to her. Then she remembered what the judge had said. She was going to a prison too. Georgie looked at the three of them as they entered the bus.

"I don't think so." The bigger of the three of them told her that they could do this the easy way or the hard way. "Hard way. I don't want to go to prison for over a year, waiting on my trial. You go back in there and tell him whatever it takes to have him change his mind. But I'm not getting off this bus."

"The hard way it's going to be then." He pulled out a gun and pointed it at her. When long electrical things came out of it, she knew she was going to be tazed. Christ, oh mighty, she hated that.

She couldn't move her body at all. Her mouth was open in a scream that never surfaced for anyone to hear it. If the smells were any indications she not only pissed herself but shit in her pants as well. Nothing was moving on her body, and they picked her up and pulled her out of her seat after unshackling her.

Bits and pieces came to her when she was tossed into the back seat of a cruiser. There was plastic all over the place like they'd planned her being tazed so she could shit her pants. She remembered them telling her, or at least someone, that she'd be easier to deal with. Even though they were right, it didn't mean she wasn't pissed off too.

By the time the car was slowing down, she was able to sit up, but didn't care for that so much. Her pants were dirty, and sitting in them made her slightly sick. Georgie was going to get these bastards when she got out, and she'd show them what it felt like to have dirty pants on. All of the fuckers.

"Welcome home, Georgetta Jameson." She looked at the walls of the big prison and thought that there wouldn't be any comfort in being here. She'd be lucky if they gave her a mattress. She knew this place better than her own home, having spent the last ten years here on a trumped-up murder conviction.

Before going inside, she was stripped down to her girly parts hanging out and hosed off. The water tore at her skin and hurt a great deal, but it wasn't until they had her bend over and spread her cheeks that the real pain started. She knew that she had shit herself again when the laughter was there. Georgie was going to be the laughingstock of the whole prison system if she didn't miss her bet.

Instead of giving her a towel to dry off with, she had to stand in line to get her bunk things as well as a uniform. She remembered how the last time she was in prison, how the ugly green had clashed with her skin color. Not that she cared about that, but it was just one more thing to be made fun of about. And Georgie hated to be teased about herself.

She thankfully didn't have a bunkmate. Having her choice of which bed she wanted wasn't as thrilling as fighting someone for the one that she'd wanted. Getting onto the top bunk after dressing herself and finger-combing her hair, she was ready to call it a day. However, the system has other plans for her.

Being asked to step out of her cell, she realized that she was in time to get dinner. Depending on what day of the week it was, it determined what the meal was going to be. She didn't remember them right off the bat, but she did know that Friday's was fish. The most disgusting thing on the menu by far.

Since she didn't have a crew yet, she was fine sitting by herself at one of the long tables. Keeping her head down and not looking around were other things she remembered about this place. Making eye contact with the wrong person was dangerous. Georgie was able to choke down the two pieces of fish by soaking them up in the gravy — fish gravy, she supposed — and swallowing them whole. Christ, what she wouldn't give for a nice can of beer right about now.

"You too good for us?" Grunting out an answer, she peeked from beneath her eyelashes where the guards were hanging out. It was too far for her to expect any help from them. "I asked you a question. You too good to sit with us or what?"

"I just got here. I don't know anyone yet." She was told that was a poor excuse. "Well, I don't know anyone here yet, I'm just making my way, that's all. I don't want any trouble."

"Did I say anything about you being in trouble, bitch? I asked you why you're sitting there all by your lonesome when there are all kinds of friends you can make here. Or are you the shit woman? That's it. You shit yourself and now no body wants to sit with you. You're Stinky Pete, aren't you? That's what we're going to call you from now on. Stinky Pete."

"No, you're not." She stood up, and the pit bull inmate stood up as well. "You don't want to mess with me. I've been here before for murder and I don't fuck around."

"Watch your language, inmate." Another thing she'd forgotten was no cursing around the place. She'd have to remember the rules soon before she got herself killed. The guard walked away after telling her she was going to be in trouble with the warden if she didn't curb her language.

Pit Bull laughed and was told to sit down and finish her meal. Her yes sir, was just loud enough for him to hear but wouldn't carry across the room. Georgie was about ready to resume her own meal when someone bumped her from behind.

It took her several precious seconds to realize she'd been hurt somehow. Trying to see who had shanked her, she found that she was having a difficult time focusing. When she fell off the seat, no one came to her aid. She was surely going to die right there on the floor, and she'd only been here for a few hours.

"This is for Betsy," was whispered to her as her vision was too hard to focus on anything. Another stab to her body, and this one really hurt. "I hope you enjoy hell, bitch."

She must have passed out because when she opened her eyes, she was still on the floor, but the guards had decided to come and see what was going on. Coughing once, one of the men turned away and barked for someone to get the first aid kit. Georgie thought that she was well beyond a kit and might need someone to take her to surgery.

"Who did this to you?" The chances of her living were feeling sort of slim right now, but she'd not rat anyone out on the off chance that she did live. Not that she had any idea who had stabbed her, but she wouldn't say that either. "Did you see anyone around you?"

"Am I gonna die here? I just got here." The man said that he'd been watching her and didn't think anyone hurt her on his watch. "Yet here I am bleeding to death on the dining room floor. I didn't do this to myself, you know."

"I heard about you. I wouldn't put anything past you." He lifted his hand up to adjust his glasses, and she could see the blood all over his hands. "Christ, can someone get a doctor before she bleeds out?"

Again, she thought she had passed out because the next time she opened her eyes, she was in a bed of sorts in what looked like an emergency room. People were standing all around her, talking about someone being stabbed three times, when she must have made a noise so that they turned to look at her.

"You've been stabbed three times. Do you remember who would have done that to you? We have it on video recordings, but we can't make out their faces. We can get the person who did this to you if you can remember anything."

"Am I dying?" The man said that they'd done everything they could for her until they could get her to a bigger hospital. "Well, why am I still here?"

Coughing again, she saw the blood on her chest. She was told that they were waiting on an ambulance to take her, but that it didn't look good. They couldn't stop the bleeding. She begged them to not let her die. The man with her now shook his head and told her he was sorry.

She was weak now, like she'd had some kind of killer flu, and she'd not fully recovered from it. Then she couldn't keep her eyes open, and the voices were sounding far away. She was dying, and she couldn't do anything about it. Weaker by the minute, she asked for her brother, but no one was paying attention to her anymore. Inhaling as deeply as she could, Georgie knew she'd just drawn her last breath.

Chapter 9

Demi hung up the phone and turned to look at his little family. He and Mandy had been married just over an hour ago, and then he petitioned to adopt the boys with Mandy. They were all for it, but there was still paperwork to be filed to get things going in the right direction.

"I didn't know who they were talking about until I remembered Georgie." Martin asked him what had happened. "I'm afraid she was killed last night by another inmate. They don't know if it was two people or three. She never made it to the hospital."

"I thought you was gonna say that she escaped from the police and was coming after us. I'm glad that we don't have to worry about her anymore." Martin looked at Mandy before he continued. "I know it's not nice to hope someone dies, but she was powerful mean to Teddy and me, Momma too when she'd come around."

"I'm sorry, too, Martin, but if you can, try not to be too happy about it if someone says something to you about her dying. All right?" He nodded and said that he'd try, but was glad that she'd not be getting out again. Mandy nodded at him before continuing. "I understand, buddy."

"They want me to go to the other prison to talk to Samuel. They said that it might be better coming from a family member. I'm not related to him." Mandy pointed out that she was his sister-in-law, which would make him his brother-in-law. "I'm not sure it works like that. I think you're right in how you're related to him, but I'm not. But I'll do it so that you don't have to. There isn't anyone else."

"No, but for his kids, and I'm not sending them there to talk to him. They're sleeping better at night now. I wouldn't want to subject them to that again." He told her that she was right. "I don't know why, but if I were you, I'd take some kind of proof. Do you think they'll have a death certificate yet? Maybe wait for it to come out in the paper?"

"That might be a good idea. But before he can hear about it through some kind of grapevine. I think that's why they were rushing me to get there. So he doesn't find out some other way." He honestly didn't want to go but knew that he couldn't send Mandy. "I was given a number to call. I'll call them back and ask for a death certificate so that I have proof. Not that I think he'll recognize that as the truth."

Demi knew that as a brother and sister, they

were close. Closer he thought than he and his brothers were. They were also mean and snakes in the grass. He'd not trust either one of them with his back turned to them ever. But it had to be done, and the only thing that he could think of was that he'd have a guard with him when he got out of hand, and he was positive that the man would.

After getting off the phone the second time, the prison said that they usually expedited certificates of death so that they could be buried right away. But a postmortem had been done because of the way she'd been killed, and it would take them a day or two. Telling them that he needed something to take to her brother, the warden said that he would write up something for him that he could give to the brother. If that was all that he could get, then so be it.

His plan was to go up later today. It would take him an hour to get there, so he really needed to get a start. The warden faxed the letter that he wrote, a really good letter to his office, so that he'd have it when he wanted to leave. By two in the afternoon, he was on his way to the prison to tell Samuel that his sister had been killed and that the prison was looking into the death to see who had done it.

By the time he arrived, he'd convinced himself that all his worrying was for nothing. Samuel would be chained to whatever room he was in, and if he had to do it in a cell, then that would be between them as well. He was nervous, and he really didn't understand why. Especially after he'd gotten there and was told how it was going to be happening.

It wasn't as if they were going to allow him to be out and roaming around while he talked to him. He'd been assured that there would be guards there with them. Also, since it was a bereavement call, then it would be done in a closed room. Still with a guard on duty, but it wouldn't be scary like he was thinking. Of course, he was afraid of Samuel. He'd seen the body of his wife after he'd killed her. She'd not gone easy.

After he'd been checked for items, he was given his letter back and sent into a large room. There were mirrors on each side of the room with a table that had been cemented to the floor. On the floor were two larger-than-normal eye hooks, and one was bolted to the table. If they used those while he was in here, he'd feel much better.

Samuel was brought in, and the man looked as if he'd gone a couple of rounds with a bat himself. His lips were both busted, his right eye was swollen shut, and his hair was a mess. And he smelled. He wasn't sure what the odor was on the man, but it was bad enough that it took his breath away.

After he was locked not just to the leg irons that were on the floor but to the table as well, he sat there staring at him like he expected him to turn over something. He asked for a beer, and Demi told him that he'd not brought him anything to drink. And beer, he'd been told, was prohibited.

"Then who the fuck are you?" The guard told him to behave, and he just stared at him before turning back to him. "I don't know you from Adam. What do you want? If you're another one of those court-appointed lawyers, then I got no use for you. None of you will do what I want anyway. I want a damned beer and some magazines to look at."

"My name is Demitrius Erikson. I'm married to your wife's sister, Mandy." He knew who she was if the cursing was any indication. "I've come to talk to you about your sister Georgie Jameson."

"She get out? I hope so. Prison ain't no place for a woman. Especially as delicate as she is. What you have to say about her?" He told him how she'd been killed. "That's not funny, you bastard. Coming here to get me riled up is what you've done. Why would you say something like that?"

"I'm not lying to you, Samuel. Nor am I trying to rile you up. Georgie was killed last night at the women's prison she was at. They don't know who did it, but they've assured me that they're looking into it using all their resources. She was stabbed three times." Samuel snatched the letter from him, then, after reading it aloud, he wadded it up and tossed it at him. Picking it up from the table, he tried again. "She was sent there to await her trial in the death of your parents. Someone was going to talk to you about their deaths as well."

"She can't be dead, I tell you. Why did someone send her to prison for? She no more deserved that than I do. And what about my kids? Where are they now that she's been carted off to prison?" He told him that he was adopting them with Mandy. "I don't want her to have them, you idiot. They're supposed to be going to my sister so that we can raise them together when I get out, and you can bet that I'm going to be getting out of here too. Where is she? My sister? Where is she right now?"

"Dead. I'm truly sorry." Samuel sat there for so long that he thought that he'd gone into a trance or something. When he finally slammed both hands down on the table, both he and the guard jumped. "Samuel, I can have the warden come here and tell you, too. But Georgie was killed last night at the federal prison where she was at. While I don't know how she—"

"You just shut up with that crap. There ain't no way that she's dead. She's a good girl, my sister is, and I won't be believing your lies about her being dead. No, I won't. Now you tell me where she is, or so help me, I'm going to come across this table and slam your head into the wall until you're dead."

The words he said were scary enough, but it was the way that he said it that terrified him. His voice didn't raise, nor did he move his hands in a way that made him be frightened of his movements; it was the very polite, soft way in which he said it. Like he was telling him that there was a movie on the television that he wanted to watch. Feeling a shiver of fear race down his spine, Demi backed away from the table and put his hands on his lap. It hadn't occurred to him how close he was to him until that moment.

"There's nothing more that I can tell you other than she was killed last evening. There will be a death certificate that I can send to you, but I don't know if you'll believe that any more than what I've already told you. She's gone." He stood up and stepped back when Samuel tried to stand as well. The guard with his hand on his weapon looked ready to pull it out and take care that Samuel was dead as well, which scared him just a little too. "You have a good life, Samuel, and I hope sometime soon you come to terms with the fact that your sister is dead."

He was out the door before he could think that he didn't know where to go. There had been too many turns and twists getting here that he wasn't sure how to leave. Just as he was ready to go back into the room, an officer came out of the room next to the one that he'd been in and escorted him out of the building. If he saw anyone on his way out, he didn't know, for his eyes were on his feet to put one foot in front of the other one to make sure he didn't fall on his way out.

By the time he made it to his car, he was sick. Leaning over, holding onto the back of his car, he threw up everything that he had for lunch. It hadn't been much, but it was enough to make him ill for several minutes after he'd tossed it all up. Leaning against his car, he left the breeze of the afternoon blow over him, making him feel less sick now that he was out in the open and more like he'd just avoided something huge with Sameul Jameson.

He'd never go back. Nor would he allow Mandy to come and visit the man either. Samuel was dangerous, and he didn't care who he killed or threatened to get what he wanted. No wonder he'd been beaten up. The man couldn't be trusted to behave himself while in prison with other inmates. How would anyone think that he'd be all right getting out to rain terror on completely innocent people that had nothing to do with him?

On the way home, he didn't feel any better about what had happened. As the miles were eaten up behind him, he thought of how it must have been for the children of his to have been around him. And poor Betsey. It's small wonder that she wasn't killed before she had been. Samuel was a monster and a deadly one at that.

He came to a decision while driving, too. He was going to tell the boys daily, if not hourly, that he loved them. Demi wanted them to know that he loved them no matter what they did. And he was going to tell Mandy that she was the love of his life too. Why would anyone want to have someone in their lives if they were going to do nothing but beat them down? To have them feel like they wished you were dead so that you'd not bother them or frighten them anymore. Why? Just why would you do that to another human being that had no more to do with being your son in that you brought them into the world for your own amusement? Demi felt his belly churn up again as he was thinking about Samuel and Betsey and those two little boys. And what would have happened to Martin and Teddy had Georgie gotten them in some sort of irrational way?

She would have been no better than her brother. Using them for government assistance rather than loving them because they'd only just lost their mom. He wasn't thrilled about Betsey either. She should have done something the first time that he hit her. Or at least tried. Talking to Mandy about her, she was getting abused even before the boys came along, and knew what sort of person her husband was. Some people he only just come to realize shouldn't ever have children.

They didn't deserve them.

~*~

Mandy was able to get this week's class off to a good start. With Demi coming around and helping out, it seemed to flow a good deal faster, too. With the boys back in school, it was lonely around the house even though she had plenty of things to do. It wasn't the same without them around all the time.

"Did you get the lists for the schools?" She handed the lists off, six in total, for what each class would need in the way of supplies for the rest of the year. "Good. We'll get them water too unless that's already on the list."

"It's not on all of them, but it is on the second grade as well as the fifth grade classes. If you don't mind me saying, I think some of the teachers are asking for things that are well out of the classroom projects. Like one of them asked for fifty headphones. Why so many when the kids were to bring in one each when the school year started? Also, there are things like paper towels as well as tissues. There are more than I think necessary on the lists. Almost like each kid could take home three boxes each for the entire school and still have leftovers."

"I'll look into that. Sometimes I feel like we're supplying things for their homes, too, and that's not what we're doing." Alex looked over the list. "Why do they need a microwave for the second graders. Last I heard, they didn't have eating in their rooms. And I know for a fact that the teachers' lounge has a nice one." She looked over more of the lists. "It says here gift cards so that they can buy supplies not on the list. I thought that was what we did this for. So they'd not have to buy things that are listed."

"I think you're being taken advantage of." Alex sat down with the list and told her a couple more things that she'd found. "Wait until you get to the sixth grade. They want paint to paint their rooms during Christmas break this year when it comes up. This is only the third week. Why does it need to be painted already?"

"I'm going to have to get some clarification on these. There is no way they're going to need this much in the way of supplies to get them through the end of the year. There are things on here that I know for a fact are just things that the teachers lounge has had put in." She started making a list. "This is stupid. I'm going to tell them not to do this if this is the way they're going to be treating the charity that comes their way. Did you see this list from the front office? I didn't know that we had anything to do with supplying them things?"

"Ms. Lavine handed me that when I was leaving. She said that it's only a few things that they're forever running out of. I don't see how that's something that, as a charity, we should be responsible for either. I mean, since when do we supply them with tissues and wipes too? And why so many?" The two of them made a list with the counts of what they were requesting. There were over two hundred and fifty boxes of tissues as well as three hundred containers of wipes. That didn't even count the fifty-five containers for the front office and the hundred boxes of tissues. "I really think this is wrong in so many ways."

By the time they were finished, they had three microwaves, two televisions, as well as a stereo system for one of the rooms. There were things on the list like paper napkins and paper plates. And then there were the water bottles that they wanted. Over three hundred and seventy-five cases, not individual bottles but cases of water for the rooms that requested them. This was just ridiculous.

"I wonder where they'd even store that much water. And they can't even say it's for the band boosters. We already supply them with water at every home game to sell. I'm going to have to have a meeting with these teachers. I'm curious as to what they'll say when we ask them what on earth they were thinking about when they put these things on the list. I'm betting, as you said, they're taking most of this home with them." Locke came into the room when they were totaling up the price it would be for the things on the lists. "You're not going to believe these lists that Mandy picked up today. We're supplying them with things that aren't even part of the teachers' programs for school. Look at these."

As Locke went over the lists, she and Alex talked about what they'd actually give them. She was of the opinion that they didn't need anything from them if they were going to be greedy but Alex said it would be better if they just got them a few things then told them they were shit out of luck for the rest.

"I'm going to put my foot down to the principal. There is no way that he knows about these lists. And if he does, then shame on him, too. This is something out of a book, people taking advantage of the rich people in town because they think that they're stupid or something. Having money doesn't make you blind to people taking advantage of you. I'm going to call Zander to let him know about this and have him talk to the principal. Something needs to be done about this." They both agreed. "Don't buy anything yet. I want to see what's going on with this first."

"All right. The second-grade teacher did ask me how quickly she could get the gift cards. She said that paint is on sale right now, and she wanted to pick it up. Do you suppose she's painting her home with charity money?" Locke said that he hoped not, that would get her into deep trouble using charity money fraudulently. "I think that they all are using it that way.

We need to crack down on this before it gets really out of hand. Next, they'll be asking us for new desks or something."

"We are helping with the new school. Not in the way of financial needs, but with people working with the contractors to get it done quickly. They get a great deal of money to have a new school built, as well as the things that would go into it." She asked Locke if he was sure about that. "I'm not sure now that I've seen these. Let me call Zander and see what he has to say about this. If he goes to the school, I might go with him. I want, like you two, to see the reaction of the people when they find out we're not going to do this."

Zander was pissed off about it. Locke put the call on speaker so that they could hear how upset he was. After reading him a couple of things on the list, he was furious about the way they were taking advantage of the group of them. He made an appointment as soon as today to talk to the other man.

The meeting was going to take place as soon as Zander could get there. The principal, Mr. David Sheen, said that he didn't know what was going on, but he didn't want it to fester and become something serious, and asked them to come in now. Since he didn't want the teachers to know what was going on, they asked him to come to the Crockery Pot to have lunch and talk there. The man was more than agreeable. She and Alex were going too just to be there in case they wanted information about the lists. Also, to see if he was a part of it, which they all hoped that he wasn't.

David showed up just as they were being seated. He was a good-looking younger man, but also had a serious look about him. Mandy was impressed that he brought himself a notepad and pen to take notes. She noticed that there were a couple of lines on his paper before they even began. He asked to go first.

"I don't know why, but I was asked to see if there would be gift cards coming soon. This is from Ms. Piper, the second-grade teacher. She's been with us a year now and perhaps doesn't understand that you supply us with things rather than give out gift cards to let them spend the money. I might be wrong about that; I'm just not sure I ever heard of it happening." Zander handed the man the list from Ms. Piper's class without saying a word. As he went over it, his face got redder and redder as he got to the bottom. "I don't understand what it is I'm looking at. Or perhaps I do, and I'm just shocked by it. I don't know where they would have gotten the idea that—is this from my office? What do they need a microwave for? We have two now that are seldom used."

David was fired up by the time he had gone over the lists with Zander. He told him that if this was how they were going to treat the charity that supplied them with extra, they just might not do it next year. David asked him to allow him to talk to the teachers. He'd get it to stop.

"What are you going to do?" David said he was going to find out who thought that this was a good idea, then go from there. "And if they don't tell you whose idea it is, then what are you going to do? To be honest with you, sir, my family isn't at all happy with these lists. It sounds as if we're supplying them with things that, at the end of the year, will go home with them, if not before then. These lists total up to being more than eleven grand. We don't even spend that much on the backpacks that we donate with all these supplies and more in them."

"I would ask you to hold off on buying anything for a while. I might even have you not buy anything at all for this school year. But it won't come back on you guys. I promise you that this is going to be laid at their feet and they'll know too that I'm pissed off as well." He looked over the lists again. "This isn't even a couple of teachers here. This is all of them. Every teacher has put things on the list that shouldn't be there."

David was going to set up a meeting for this coming Friday. It would satisfy him on so many levels to have them stay after classes on Friday to talk to them. Hoping for a long weekend, he'd have them an answer to their lists then. Mandy thought that Daivd was looking forward to this as much as they were pissed off about it. She could almost feel sorry for the teachers who had given her the lists that they thought would amount to about five hundred dollars total, not the lists that they got.

By the next morning, word had gotten around about the teachers' meeting the next evening. Gossip traveled quickly, and since Daivd had told them it was about the Erikson's donations to the school, there was speculation that everything that they'd put onto their lists was going to come to them at the meeting. Some were even suggesting that they bring help with moving the stuff they had asked for into storage, which they expected the charity to pay for as well.

She and Zander, since she'd gotten the lists, were going to be there. He was already drafting a lawsuit on the things that they thought the teachers were going to be using for their own homes. No one would ever believe that they wanted that much water for the classrooms for the school year.

When the meeting was to start, she noticed that there were a lot of trucks and vans in the parking lot, like a great many of them for moving things. A great many of the teachers had changed into jeans and T-shirts with tennis shoes to work. It was going to be epic to see their faces when he told them that they weren't getting anything.

The next afternoon, just yesterday, David had called Zander and told him that the school wouldn't be needing their help for the rest of the school year. The more he had thought about it, the angrier he'd gotten, and he decided that they'd have to do without if they were going to be greedy. He even had him fill out a lawsuit for each teacher that stated that they were fraudulently using things that had been donated for their own personal use.

"I heard them talking about how they had pulled the wool over your eyes about the lists. I know now that the gift cards for the paint was going to Ms. Applet for her daughter's bedroom and the kitchen. As was the microwave that she asked for on her list." David sighed heavily. "I'm ashamed to admit that I had no idea this was going on. And to be honest with you, I didn't think that this would happen for as much as you've donated to the schools in the past. I'd tell you to go to another school to help out instead of this one, but I know that without the donations, the regular donations, this school wouldn't be in half as good of shape as it is right now. I doubt very much we'd be getting the new building that is going up as we speak."

"I'm sorry as well, David. We won't cut you off completely, but we won't be donating anything to the teachers' funds this year. Also, the end of year awards dinner, either." He said it was no less than he expected. "The kids aren't at fault, so we'll continue with the backpack funds, but I'm doubtful that unless something really changes, we'll be giving any more money to the school."

"Would you mind if I told them that?" Zander had told him that he was going to be saying that at the meeting. "Good. I want them to come to the realization that they've bitten the very hand that has fed them. I mean, I expected you to tell me that your family isn't going to be helping with breakfast anymore."

"As I said, this has nothing to do with the students. We'd not take that from them. But the teachers are going to have to pay for their meals from it." David asked if the teachers were eating too. "They are. All of them."

"Christ, there is no end to what they'll do, is there? All right." They made arrangements to get together on what was going to be said and done at the meeting, and now here they were. Zander had even dressed up in a three-piece suit, and she in a professionally looking suit herself. This was going to be something completely unexpected for everyone there.

Chapter 10

Zander looked around the room at the fourteen teachers. Each of them had given a list as to what they wanted for their rooms, and the list had been outrageously expensive. One had wanted a high-tech microwave, and another insisted that they pick up the brand of water that they specified on the list. One hundred and twenty cases of the more expensive water, too. In the sixteen ounce bottle size, that would be two pallets of water with a whopping seventy-two cases per. Where were they going to store that sort of purchase? In their rooms? He was going to find out today.

Who had told the other teachers to pad their list? He had a feeling that he knew who had done it and why they'd called Alex last night and given a list that was more in line with what they'd been expecting. He wanted the others to get into trouble. Or he'd thought about what he'd done and decided that he'd be the odd teacher out when it came to how much money they were asking for. He'd bet his last check against the fact that he'd told them all that the Erikson Foundation men were too stupid to look over the list as anything but a nice list of things to put into their rooms. Well, he was going to enjoy this more than he probably should.

Now that he had a good list of who they were, David helping him out with the way they were seated, he was ready as he'd ever be with taking the teachers down a few notches. He thought that David, too, was going to have fun. Firing them all is what he'd do, but then he was hard like that. They tried their best to screw over a foundation that was helping them more with class funds than any other school in the country. David stood up, and the room quieted.

"Today we're here to talk about the latest lists that you handed over to Mandy Erikson when she was here this week. Zander wants to go over some of the things on the list with you." There was a slight discomfort in the room. They shifted in their seats and suddenly had to look at their shirts or blouses. None of them made eye contact with any of them. "He just wants to make sure that you understand what it is that you've requested is going to take up room in your classes. Mrs. Raider, I believe you're first."

"Why do I have to be first?" He pointed out that she was the first one in the seats. "Oh. Well, I don't want to go first. Go on to someone else and let me gather my thoughts on the things."

"You ordered to have one hundred and fifty cases of water for your room, is that right?" Zander asked her to stand up. "I just wanted to make sure that you understand that's going to be two or more pallets of water stacked pretty high. Where do you plan to keep the extras until they're needed? I mean, you only have twenty-four students, and if you count you and your aid, that's less than a case a day if you only get one bottle. You're going to be a while before you get to the other hundred-plus cases."

"I'll have a storage unit. I was planning on putting things in there that are too many for the classroom." He asked her where it was, so that they could make sure that things were put there. "Oh, it's near to my home. That way, I can pick up a couple of cases when I need them. That's what I'm going to do. I never thought of them being so many and large."

"I didn't realize that you'd be paying for a unit. That must be expensive at what? Thirty-something a month? My brother had one, he said it nearly drained him in keeping up with the payments each month." She said she thought that the foundation would pick up the tab. "No, I'm afraid not. And once it's put into your storage locker, we won't have anything to do with it. You'll be on your own."

"What do you mean, I'll be on my own?" He told her. "I never thought of it freezing or getting too hot in the summer. I thought that…well, I don't know what I thought."

"Along with the other things that you got, the fifty cases of tissues. Do the kids in your room have a lot of colds? Or perhaps allergies? This would be another pallet of tissues for your room. In total, you would have to rent out three storage units to hold all the extra things that you have on your list. At that price, you'd be paying over a hundred dollars a month for just storage." She looked confused, and he smiled. He knew that it was his prey-to-predator kind of smile, and he used it all the time in the courtroom. "Here we are trying to save you money and—"

"Mr. Carter told us that you were too stupid to notice how much we were getting and that you'd blindly give it to us. We were told that you'd never check and we could—"

"Me? I don't know what you're talking about. I didn't say anything about padding the list. I simply went along with the rest of you until last evening." He looked at him. "You got my revised list, didn't you? None of my things are going to have to be put into storage. I gave them a good list. Isn't that right, Mr. Erikson?"

"You did. However, I think that things happened just the way that they said. While I have no proof of your wrongdoing, I do believe what they say is true. You were behind all this." He said he'd better take that back. "I will when it's proven to me that you had nothing to do with this. And just so you all know, using donated things from a charity for your own personal gain is against the law. Padding these lists sounds like something that you're doing, like the refrigerator and the microwave. Paint for your room. Pallets of things like bottled water. It all sounds to me like you were doing this for your own personal use."

It was a free-for-all, all in them blaming Carter and trying to say that they'd take a great deal less than they'd been told to pad their lists with. Even Carter was saying that he'd redo his list again just to prove that he'd had nothing to do with the way the other teachers had done their lists. Finally having enough, David let go of a whistle that rivaled Shipley's when she was trying to get someone's attention.

"Sit down and shut up." They did it immediately, not even in the chairs they'd been in before. "I tell you what is going to happen right now. There will be no more help from the Eriksons for the next ten years or until you quit or I fire you. And yes, you have no idea how close I am to firing each and every one of you for this mess."

"You can't fire us for padding something that we were given to list for them." He told Ms. Applet to watch him. "This is ridiculous. Who will you have teach these brats? The Eriksons? Sure, go right ahead, and I'll tell the board what you've been up to. And even if I have to make it up, you'll be on the next bus out of town by the time I'm finished with you."

The board had been there all the time. In the hallway, listening to what transpired in the meeting. After they were introduced to the group, they sat down in the room right behind each teacher. Now things were going to get interesting. Ms. Applet stood up and turned to the board.

"I was upset. I didn't mean that about David. I've been accused of taking things for my own personal use from a charity when all I wanted to do was get some nice things for the classroom for the kids." One of the board members, he didn't know their names, just then said that she'd called them brats before. Even from where he was sitting, he could tell that her face had turned a dark red in embarrassment. "I feel as if we've all been ambushed in this. How were we to know that they didn't want us to order things for the kids for the rest of the year?"

"Ms. Applet, your list was the most padded. You had on there that you wanted three hundred cases of water, seventy-five cases of tissues, as well as a plethora of other things that we don't supply to the school at all, like plastic silverware, napkins, paper towels, and paper plates. I also know that at the end of the summer, you and your family have a hog roast that supplies all those things to everyone who comes. You were taking things from us that would have supplied all the extras that you'd need for that, I believe." She lifted her chin up but said nothing. "Also, there are things on here like tubs—you gave the sizes that you wanted as well."

"I thought of the kids." He pulled up her list, naming off all the things on it as well as how many she wanted. "Oh hell. So what? It's not like you guys don't have all the money. You can well afford all the things on our lists twice over. I don't know what you're bitching about. It's not like I asked you for the hogs to go along with the other stuff. I'll admit it, yes, it's for my own personal use. What are you going to do to me? Fire me? I was looking for another job when I found this one. Go ahead. Do your worst on me. But try to find a teacher this late in the year."

Mrs. Rider from the board handed her a thick envelope, and she was escorted out by a security team that he'd had no idea had been brought in. After that, all the teachers were escorted out one by one for their month off without pay. It would hurt a great many of them, being off work without any income, but that had nothing to do with him. He'd only been brought in to prove a point, and he doubted any of them got it.

As they were sitting there, talking amongst themselves, he had an idea that David hadn't known of the layoffs nor that anyone was going to be fired. He looked as poleaxed as he felt, knowing that the town was going to find out about their part in the firing and laying off of all the teachers at the elementary school. There would be a lot of uproar about it. Some backlash as well. But he'd done what needed to be done to keep the charity afloat without being drained by a bunch of people who had decided to take advantage of them.

For the rest of the evening, he decided to go to the football game that was playing at home this week. He'd only been there ten minutes when he was approached by two different people about the rumor that the teachers had been given a month off without pay and that the charity foundation was no longer going to supply things for the teachers.

"I have to tell you, Zander, I depend on you guys to help my family out. I have five kids in the school right now, and without you guys supplying them with backpacks full of the things they need, I don't know what we'd do. You can bet that they'd not have anything that's for sure." He assured the man that the backpacks would still be supplied. But nothing to the teachers who had gotten greedy. "I heard about them lists. Can't say that I blame the board for getting rid of them. Shameful is what that was. Just shameful. People like them, well, you can bet that I'm not going to be feeling sorry for them. Durn shame that they had to bite the hand that fed them."

"Thank you for that. I wasn't sure how the town would react knowing what my part in this was going to be." He told him that there would be complainers all over the place, but he wasn't to pay them any mind. "I won't. Thank you so much."

He ended up not staying for the game. Zander had to defend himself a couple of times, but mostly everyone was worried about how it was going to affect the backpack donations that they did every year. He'd not realized how many people really depended on that donation to the school. Spending the rest of his evening at home, he was glad for the extra time that he could go over his notes for the upcoming trial for Carrie's family. They'd hit her one too many times as far as he was concerned.

~*~

Demi was watching the kids while Mandy was working on her classes. She'd been doing them so long now that she was getting really good at them. And he knew that people appreciated her ability at making it easier on them when they learned a new skill. He knew that ordering groceries online had saved them a lot of time and energy.

"What time is Mandy supposed to be home? I have a question for her." Demi asked if he could answer it. "No, it has to be her. But I have one for you, too. The kids at school make fun of me on account of me not having any parents. Can I call you, Dad? It sure would keep me from being beat up every day."

"Are you really being beat up every day, Teddy?" He said he wasn't, but they did make fun of him without a dad or mom. "I don't care if you call me dad or not, but I want you to want that instead of being pressured into it."

"Nobody is making me say that. I just want to have a dad that is real. Not like my other dad when he'd beat us — and he really did beat us all the time." Demi told him he was sorry about that. "Why do grown-ups say that all the time? They're sorry that my real dad beat me up all the time. If they was sorry, they should do something about it when it's happening. Telling me you're sorry is too late to help me."

Teddy was angry, and he didn't understand why. Before he could get to the bottom of it, Teddy burst into tears and flung himself into his arms. He kept saying that he was sorry that he didn't have someone to love him when he was littler. That he was always looking for someone to smack him around, and how exhausting it was. There were other things, too. He missed his momma and that he didn't think she did a good job in keeping them safe, not like he and Mandy did. The poor kid was so upset when he looked up at him that it did something painful to his heart.

"You mad at me?" Demi asked him why he

thought he should be mad at him. "I'm a sobby babe that cries a lot. My dad would have hit me into next week if I'd done that around him."

"Do you want me to hit you into next week?" He shook his head. "Yeah, I'm glad. I don't know how hard that would have to be, but I'm pretty sure that I'd feel worse than you about it. I don't ever want to hit you for any reason."

"Even when I'm bad?" Demi told him they'd cross that bridge when they came to it. "All right. I will try my best not to tempt you into hitting me then."

"Good idea." He held the little boy until his small tremors stopped. "Let's talk about what you said, all right? Your father was a mean bastard who didn't deserve you or Martin. You understand that, don't you?" He said that he did. "Then why do you think your mother didn't do a good job in keeping you safe from him?"

"She'd hide behind us when he was in the mood." That was something that he didn't know about Betsey. It made his opinion of her lower even more. "She used to tell on us, too. Like if we did something bad—sometimes I think she was making things up to get us in trouble with him. Like once she told him that I'd spilled some milk and didn't clean it up. I never had no milk to spill. And I'd of cleaned it up right now instead of waiting until dad came home to beat me. But she did that all the time."

"You do know that if you spill milk around here and I know you've had some, you'd better clean it up right away, too." He said he'd do that too on account of him not being in trouble here with that. "No, I'd not beat you for spilling milk unless you did it on purpose. Which I don't see you doing."

"No, I'm not no dummy." He'd correct his English later when the conversation wasn't so serious. "She'd hit on us too sometimes for nothing or no reason. Once I got home from school, Martin and me were telling her something that happened in the lunch room. She smacked us both so hard for talking that my head hit the table and hurt for a week. There was no reason for that."

Demi started to answer the boy when he looked up and saw Mandy standing in the doorway. She made a gesture for him not to tell Teddy she was there, and he nodded once. Teddy's back was to the door, so he'd not see her at all unless he got up from the floor.

"There was this one time I brought her home a pretty flower that I picked in the yard. It wasn't belonging to anyone, I wouldn't take someone's pretty flowers, but I gave it to her, and she just threw it in the trash can, telling me that she didn't care for dead things in her house. That it was bad enough that she had little boys around that messed things up for her.

I don't think she liked us all that much. Not like you and Mandy do. I could pick her weeds and she'd bawl like a baby, putting them in the prettiest vase she has. She'd even tell everyone that I'd picked it for her like it was a fancy rose or something." He cocked his head before speaking again. "When she does stuff like that, it makes my heart feel good. Like she's touched it with her fingers and put a smiley face on it. Don't tell her that. She'll think I'm loopy or something."

"I promise I won't tell her." There were other incidents like those. He'd gotten into the habit of tossing away his papers if they had a good grade on them. She'd then ask him if he was trying to show her how stupid she was. Another incident involved flowers, and they stopped bringing home flowers from a Mother's Day project from school. Mostly, he thought that Teddy was confused by his mother's treatment of them. He didn't understand his father either, but he wasn't loopy around them one minute, then mean the next.

Teddy talked himself out and fell asleep on his chest. It was all he could do not to go and find Betsey's grave and give her hell for what she'd done. He wondered now if that was the reason they'd never asked to go to her grave. They never wanted to go and visit her and take flowers. Now he thought he knew why.

Mandy had been crying when she came into the room. Sitting in a chair across from him and Teddy, she asked him how much she'd missed. He told her about the flowers and the other things that Teddy had told him about. She said she'd heard it all then. And it broke her heart.

"I remember Betsey being so mean to me when I was a child. She'd tell mom lies, too, so that I'd get into trouble. Then she'd come into my room, read me a story and hug me and kiss me like she'd not just gotten my butt whipped for her lies." She leaned back in the chair. "I think I was making her out to be the victim when all along I knew she was almost as bad as Sameul was, if not worse. He was at least consistently mean to them. She sounded like she was just as he said, loopy."

"I wonder if Martin has some stories about her, too. He was home with her when Teddy was in preschool. I don't imagine that he had any better time with her than poor Teddy did." Mandy shook her head and cried a bit more. "I'm so sorry, honey, that you had to find out this way."

"No, this was fine. I'm just glad that he was able to go to you with it. You said he wanted to call us mom and dad. I'm all right with that. It certainly will be easier on them if they do that. I mean, having to explain how I'm their aunt and that my sister was their mother, but she was killed by their father, who's in prison, but you're just married to me. It's complicated."

"When you put it like that, yes, it is." Martin joined them in the living room and asked if Teddy was all right. He was only supposed to be gone for a minute and didn't return. "He had some things to get off his chest. Do you know what that means?"

"Yeah, he's been pondering stuff for a while now. It keeps him up at night wondering about silly stuff." Martin climbed up into Mandy's lap. "I'm going to take me a nap too. I'm pooped out."

Martin must have been because in less time than he would have thought, the little boy was snoring softly and holding onto his aunt. It lured him to sleep, too, the way the warm body was against his. The soft sounds of breathing. Before he knew it, Demi was dozing off, and no matter how hard he tried to stay awake, the faster sleep seemed to pull at him.

When he woke, he was alone on the couch but had a light blanket over him. He didn't move for a while, just realizing how much he must have needed the nap when Teddy came in to check on him, he said.

"I'm fine. I must have been exhausted myself." He decided not to mention their talk unless Teddy did. "Would you like to get some supper out tonight? It's the cook's night off, and we could go into town to get something?"

"Not pizza." He laughed, telling him he was all

right with that, too. "I like it better when we make it at home. It's hotter, and we have fun making them. But we eat it a lot."

"We do at that." Sitting up, he realized how late it was. "Tell Mandy and Martin what we're doing, and I'll warm up the car. It got chilly today after the sun went down."

After Teddy left him, Demi stood up and stretched. He was going to have to hit the gym a bit more as he felt out of shape, and he'd not felt that way since he'd been a kid. Going to get some clean clothes on, he was halfway up the stairs when Mandy came out of the bedroom. Pulling her into his arms when she joined him on the stairs, he told her how much he loved her and loved everything about her.

"Everything? I mean, even my little boobs?" He told her they were perfect as far as he was concerned. "You're just trying to get laid."

"Of course I am. I'm a man, aren't I? That's all we think about is getting laid, and even when we do, we're thinking about the next time and the next. We're creatures of habit, and all we want and think about is sex. Sex. Sex."

She was saved from answering him by the kids coming down the hallway. They were running down the stairs when he kissed her again, much to the amusement of the kids. As they were loading up in the car, he was teasing them about someday wanting to kiss girls, and Martin said that he'd not ever be ready, but Teddy told him that girls were all right so long as they weren't mad at you.

"They sure can be powerful mad at you when they think you've done something wrong. You don't even have to do it, they just get all skank eye at you and you can't tell them anything." He asked if that had happened to him. "Nah, but I've seen it happen. She hollered at him, but good too. I don't think it's right to hit on somebody that you're mad at. I'd never hit anyone unless it's the only way I can save myself. I've been hollered at enough for three kids my age."

The rest of the trip was the boys telling them stories about school and how the teachers were all gone off for a month, and they had subs. Martin liked his substitute teacher, but Teddy said that all his did was play on her phone and ignore them.

"She said that she really didn't want to be a teacher but liked having summers off. She'd not planned on getting a job until she was twenty-five. Her parents are paying for everything while she's off." Teddy sure knew enough about his teacher for it only being one day with her. "Oh, and get this. She said that if anyone of us got sick and puked on the floor, we was going to have to clean it up. I told Mr. David, our principal, about it, and he told me that he'd take care of it. I had to clean up puke once, it's not anything that I'd want to do ever again."

They never brought up their parents, but Teddy did call him dad once. It was a feeling that he thought he could live with forever. Martin called Mandy mom twice more since they'd left the house, and since they'd not made a big deal out of it, he wouldn't either. However, it was a great deal to him, and he loved it.

Pulling into their favorite pasta restaurant, he decided that he'd enjoy this too. He could make anything on their menu without a thought, but he wasn't cooking tonight, and he was fine with picking up the bill for this. Everyone was happy, and that's all he really cared about.

By the time they were finished eating, the boys getting much better at ordering their own food, he was ready for another nap. Carbs did that to him, and he'd had plenty of them tonight. After getting dessert of fried ice cream, he was sure they were going to need to pull over so that he could sleep off the meal. Just as he was going to suggest a hotel for the night, he was that exhausted. Mandy asked if she could drive. He nearly put them in a ditch trying to get off the road so that she could take over.

"I've not been sleeping all that much at night." He wiggled his brows at her, and she laughed. Teddy wanted to know why he wasn't sleeping all that well, and he had to tell him that it was Mandy's fault. She was forever kissing on him and making things hard for him. That got him a good smack on the chest, but it was all in fun. He felt better not driving and could stay awake, not having to concentrate on the road as much as he had before.

"I was thinking about a nice vacation. Where should we all go?" He turned and put the question to the kids. They'd never been anywhere on any sort of holiday, and he wanted to be there when they saw things for the first time. Like the ocean or a roller coaster. Their first hotel stay. He was more excited about that than he thought any vacation spot could give him.

"We've never been anywhere, but I'd like to go and see things around our state. There is lots of history our teacher told us." Then getting a camper to do all those things hit him, and he mentioned it to the kids. "That would be epic. Do you think we could get one of those driving kinds? You know where we can sit on our seats while going down the road. I'd love that."

For the rest of the ride home, that is all they could talk about. A camping trip around their own state. He'd been living in Tennessee for over thirteen years now, and he'd not been to see any of the sites. Demi decided he was going to price motorhomes and have a blast with his little family. Yes, he thought to himself. This was the way life was supposed to be. Family around you when you needed them most.

Before You Go...

HELP AN AUTHOR

write a review

THANK YOU!

Share your voice and help guide other readers to these wonderful books. Even if it's only a line or two, your reviews help readers discover the author's books so they can continue creating stories that you'll love. Log in to your favorite retailer and leave a review. Thank you.

AWARD WINNING, BESTSELLING AUTHOR

Kathi Barton, a winner of the Pinnacle Book Achievement Award and a best-selling author on Amazon and All Romance books, lives in Nashport, Ohio, with her husband, Paul. When not creating new worlds and romance, Kathi and her husband enjoy camping and going to auctions. She can also be seen at county fairs with her husband, an artist and potter.

Her muse, a cross between Jimmy Stewart and Hugh Jackman, brings her stories to life for her readers in a way that has them coming back time and again for more. Her favorite genre is paranormal romance, with a great deal of spice. You can visit Kathi online and drop her an email if you'd like. She loves hearing from her fans. aaronskiss@gmail.com.

Follow Kathi on her blog: http://kathisbartonauthor.blogspot.com/